ᛈᛖᚨᚾᚢᛏ ᛒᚢᛏᛏᛖᚱ ᚨᚾᛞ ᚲᚺᚨᛟᛊ

(Peanut Butter and Chaos)

Yellow Dog
Great Plains Publications
320 Rosedale Avenue
Winnipeg, MB R3L 1L8
www.greatplains.mb.ca

Great Plains Publications gratefully acknowledges the financial support provided for its publishing program by the Government of Canada through the Canada Book Fund; the Canada Council for the Arts; the Province of Manitoba through the Book Publishing Tax Credit and the Book Publisher Marketing Assistance Program; and the Manitoba Arts Council.

Design & Typography by Relish New Brand Experience
Printed in Canada by Friesens

Library and Archives Canada Cataloguing in Publication

Title: Peanut butter and chaos / Anita Daher.
Names: Daher, Anita, 1965- author.
Description: Series statement: The mythic adventures of Samuel Templeton ; 1
Identifiers: Canadiana (print) 20220142122 | Canadiana (ebook) 20220142130 | ISBN 9781773370774 (softcover) | ISBN 9781773370781 (ebook)
Classification: LCC PS8557.A35 P43 2022 | DDC jC813/.6—dc23

TREES	WATER	ENERGY	SOLID WASTE	GREENHOUSE GASES
4	300	2	13	1,640
FULLY GROWN	GALLONS	MILLION BTUs	POUNDS	POUNDS

Environmental impact estimates were made using the Environmental Paper Network Paper Calculator 4.0. For more information visit www.papercalculator.org

Canada

THE MYTHIC ADVENTURES OF
SAMUEL TEMPLETON

BOOK ONE:
PEANUT BUTTER AND CHAOS

BY ANITA DAHER

CHAPTER ONE

SAM'S ABSOLUTELY OFFICIAL SCIENTIFIC EXPERIMENT

Sam was on the fence. Literally, and figuratively.

Literally because he was perched atop the whitewashed wooden fence that encircled his home, a neat, red-roofed blue bungalow with a large garden. In the garden, his father, Gordon Templeton, pinched tomato bleeders. After work and on weekends, Dad loved to putter in his garden almost more than anything.

Figuratively had nothing to do with a real fence. It meant he was on the edge of a next step he wasn't sure he should take.

His father stood with a great crack of his knees, tripped over his feet, and caught himself just before falling. Typical Dad. Gordon Templeton had many positive attributes, but coordination was not one of them.

Sam opened his notebook.

Nine Step Scientific Method
On Determining ~~Sam~~ Samuel Templeton's
Amazing Skills of Invisibility

Only his father called him Samuel, but an official experiment needed an official name. Plus, Dad was the only one who would see it.

It had all begun with a debate he and his friend Derek had last Sunday after watching the new *Starlingman vs The Chameleon* movie. Derek said the best superpower was flight. Sam insisted it was invisibility. Then it hit him.

He was invisible. He was invisible to his father.

The thought shook him as he wondered how long it had been like this. Maybe a while. Maybe a long time. Sure, they talked about school and TV shows and friends and stuff, but it was like his father was talking about one thing and thinking about something else. Sam might as well have been talking to the toaster.

When he was little, he'd done lots of things with his dad. He'd had *all* his attention. But was that true, or did he see things more clearly now because he was older?

Next month he would start grade seven, and three months after that he would be thirteen, ergo, an official teenager.

Ergo was a word smart people liked to use. It meant, *therefore.*

"You could just ask him," Derek had said.

"What would I say? Hey, Dad, is this something new or have you always been a bad parent?"

"You think he's a bad parent?"

"No, but that's what it would sound like."

Instead, he'd decided he would approach it in a language his father understood best: science. *Ergo*, his experiment. He would definitely not talk about superpowers. That was kid stuff, and at almost thirteen, it was time he stopped thinking like that and tried to be more like Dad. Especially if he wanted his attention. Besides, this kind of invisibility was something else entirely.

Dad was all about facts and science. Even gardening was about the science, like composting and insect cooperation and photosynthesizers. Sam, on the other hand, preferred reading and dreaming and drawing. He knew in his head that his father loved him, but he wanted him to *like* him too. How can you like someone you don't even see?

Sam read over his notes.

> Step Number One: The scientist must ask a testable question.
>
> Am I invisible?

He watched his father run his fingers through the leafy stalks of each plant: *pinch*, *pinch*, *pinch*.

What if Sam's experiment upset him and made things worse? That was the "on the fence" part.

It would be okay. If Dad looked upset, he'd tell him it was a joke. He would say he was trying it out for a story he wanted to write. They would laugh, Dad would tousle Sam's hair, and everything would go back to the way things used to be. He might even tell Sam that he was smart.

He wasn't. Not that he got terrible marks at school, but he clearly didn't get his smarts from his father.

> Step Number Two: Research.
>
> The scientist must use reliable information.

He'd made notes based on what he'd seen with his own eyes. He was his own "eyewitness." Pretty reliable.

Step Number Three: Hypothesis

My father doesn't see me watching him, ergo, I am invisible.

People like his father used *ergo* in conversation. Sam knew the word because he read a lot. Ergo, he could sound smart even if he wasn't.

Step Number Four: Create a Plan.
Step Number Five: Conduct a Fair Test.
Step Number Six: Make Observations.

Planned, tested and observed. Every day since Monday he'd watched his father garden-putter after work. On Saturday and now Sunday morning he'd watched him dig and pinch. It was like Dad's brain was somewhere else, but that was normal in the yard. Gardening had always been his "unplug" time. What wasn't normal was that lately he was like that all the time. It's weird to walk right in front of someone, think they are looking at you, but they don't blink or smile or speak or anything at all. It's like they're looking someplace else.

Or you are invisible.

A rattle and *chunk* announced the arrival of a bicycle.

"Good afternoon, Thyla," Dad called. "How are you today?"

Thyla Smith was not invisible, nor were any other neighbours who just happened by. But when Dad talked to Thyla it bugged him.

"Pretty fine, Mr. Templeton. The hummingbirds were busy today." Thyla patted the camera slung around her neck. One of Thyla's favourite things was to take pictures of birds. She was good at it. She was good at everything.

Sam was most definitely not jealous of Thyla. Nope.

Sometimes in his most private thoughts he wished she'd just disappear. People like Thyla shone so bright that others faded away.

It was annoying.

Dad went back to his gardening and Thyla flashed Sam a smile before pushing her bike into her own yard.

She had hair that reminded Sam of autumn leaves, and eyes that were the same shade of grey as a river before a storm. Thyla was both pretty and super smart, which to most people made her perfect. At sixteen, she was the youngest kid ever from Gilla Farm to start university. She could have gone anywhere with the scholarships she'd won but wanted to stay close to home and live with her mom and dad. Her first year at the University of Manitoba would begin in a few weeks.

Everyone knew Dad and Thyla were the two smartest people in Gilla Farm, which was why Mr. and Mrs. Smith asked Dad to be her tutor back when Thyla was in seventh grade.

To most people in the village, Gordon Templeton was the owner of the Playland Video Arcade, but they also knew that he used to be a neuroscience researcher at the Raynor Institute in Winnipeg. That meant he was a brain scientist.

The facts:

1. Sam was born
2. Six months later, Sam's mother and Gordon's wife, Dory Jonsdotter, moved back to Iceland and never returned.

3. Gordon Templeton quit his scientist job and moved them twenty-four minutes outside Winnipeg to Gilla Farm.

That his mother left him as soon as he was old enough to eat solid food was tragic, but he had no memory of her. Only stories. That's why he thought of her as "Dory" and not "Mom." When he was old enough to understand, Sam asked his father why he stopped being a scientist after Dory left. Dad winked and said he would always be a scientist, but that life was too short to always be so serious.

Sam didn't buy it. Gordon Templeton never played the games at his arcade, and if you looked up "serious" in a dictionary, it would show his picture.

It wasn't that he never smiled. Just not that much. Especially not lately.

Dad smiled at Thyla.

Okay, fine. Maybe Sam *was* jealous of Thyla, but he tried really hard not to feel that way. It wasn't her fault that she was perfect. It wasn't her fault that Sam was the opposite of that. Most people thought imperfect was the opposite of perfect, but Sam didn't. He thought imperfect was interesting. He thought the opposite of perfect was plain. Or invisible.

Look up "invisible" in the dictionary and it should have Sam's picture. Except you wouldn't see it, because, you know, *invisible.*

Step Number Seven: Analyze Data.
Step Number Eight: Conclusion.

Sam moved his pencil across the bottom of the page.

> *Over seven days, Dad didn't see me watching him. Yup. Totally invisible.*

There was just one more part left to do.

> Step Number Nine: Communicate and Reflect.

Sam hopped from the fence, followed his father through the side door into the kitchen, and kicked off his sneakers. Dad set his gardening clogs neatly on the mat and washed his hands under the tap before drying them on a small towel kept there for that purpose. Sam squinted at his own hands and sat.

Dad gave him a pointed look. Sam sighed, went to the sink and washed while his father set two slices of whole grain bread in the toaster, retrieved the peanut butter from the cupboard, and placed it on the counter. He pulled a butter knife from the cutlery drawer, knocked the peanut butter jar on the floor with his elbow, and retrieved it while whistling a tune that sounded vaguely like "Twinkle Little Star."

Dinner was still hours away. This was their favourite afternoon snack.

The sweet smell of the peanut butter on hot toast made his mouth water. Sam poured them each a glass of orange juice, then set the jug on what had once been Dory's special tray. Sam had always liked it, not because it was a link to his mother, but because it was made of clay and carved with a bold, inlaid Icelandic pattern that made him think of mysteries and adventure. He ran his finger along one of the eight prongs that joined in the center and fanned outward to make a circle. Each prong was crossed with three parallel strokes and had an end that looked like a rounded fork.

He'd looked it up long ago and learned it was called the *Helm of Awe*, an ancient Icelandic symbol for protection. Early Icelanders used this and other magical symbols to bring about good fortune and other wishes. Dory must have liked that pattern, because it matched his baby blanket long packed away in a chest and the embroidered cushion on a piano bench they'd finally sold at a garage sale last month.

Maybe she knew right from the start that she wouldn't come back and this was her way of saying that she wanted him to be safe. If you believed in that kind of stuff. He knew for sure that his father didn't. That wouldn't be scientific.

Dad sat, and they each bit into their toast. The clock on the wall above ticked loud as a hammer against a pot.

With butterflies batting about his belly, he shoved his notebook across the table toward his father. Dad's eyebrows bounced into sharp vees and creased in his forehead. He read the title out loud, and then blinked at Sam. "Samuel, what is this?"

Sam felt a woosh of regret and snatched it back. "It's dumb. Never mind."

His neck began to itch as Dad reached for the notebook. "I guess I can't wait for school to start, heh-heh." He swallowed and watched his father's eyes move across the top of the page. "I was practising. You know, playing around." He swallowed again.

Dad nodded but spoke as if he hadn't heard. "Excellent format. It's what you will use in seventh grade."

"I know. I copied it from Thyla's project."

Eyebrow bounce.

"I found it in your office." Sam didn't remember when Thyla had given it to Dad, only that it had been there a long time.

Dad's tutoring was the reason Thyla won the school science fair, then the regionals, and even the Canada-wide competition. Her project was about using light to activate a drug that kills cancer cells. What twelve-year-old kid even thought about stuff like cancer? Thyla had.

In personality, Thyla was a lot like Dad. Their families had lived beside each other for almost Sam's whole life. He'd never seen her making forts with friends, playing dress-up games, or soccer. She for sure never played games in the arcade. The coolest thing Sam ever saw her do was build an ant farm in her back yard.

Not that he went out of his way to see what she was doing. That would be weird. But Sam spent lots of time in his own back yard with friends, making forts, playing marbles, and kicking around a soccer ball. He'd noticed. So had his friends. So had other kids who would sometimes whisper and point. But the whispers weren't mean. Everyone liked her.

Because she was perfect.

Her parents were as normal as anyone else. Mrs. Smith was a power line technician with Manitoba Hydro and Mr. Smith was a social worker. They would have backyard barbecues and sometimes invite Sam's dad to join them. Dad would eat hamburgers and smokies cooked on the grill, but he always looked uncomfortable when other guests wanted to say more than hello. He would leave as soon as he finished eating.

"Thyla's project is a fine example," Dad said.

Sam watched as his father read line after line in his notebook, his eyes travelling across and down, across and down. Because he was super smart, Dad would surely understand what Sam was really getting at; what Sam couldn't say out loud.

Finally, he set it on the table.

Sam held his breath.

"You forgot your control," Dad said.

The room went freeze frame. Even the clock missed a beat.

"What?" Sam asked.

"Your *control*, Samuel. You need to test your hypothesis with alterations to a variable."

He swallowed. "Oh. I guess I…um…"

"Forgot?"

"Yeah," Sam said. "I guess."

His father maintained his gaze. "It's okay, son."

This was it! Dad would say that he heard Sam loud and clear, that he loved him *and* liked him. He would suggest they spend more time together, maybe go for a bike ride and get ice cream.

"Of course. You'll learn all this in seventh grade." His father returned to his toast, face neutral, his eyes looking someplace faraway inside his brain.

In Sam's gut, the peanut butter settled like a brick.

"Oh, haha, yeah. It was just a joke."

Dad looked concerned. "Science isn't a joke, Sam."

This had most definitely not gone the way he'd hoped. "I'll clean up," he said.

While Dad went out to work in his shed, probably sorting seeds for next year, Sam wiped the counter and muttered to himself. For a moment he'd had all of Dad's attention all right, but not in the way he'd wanted.

In quiet moments in the middle of the night Sam realized that there had been many troubling signs that things had changed, like not hearing when Sam asked a question, and not asking what he'd been doing in the basement for three hours. Answer: he was reading a book about the Icelandic sagas. He'd found it in a box and was so interested he'd and lost track of time.

He'd loved reading about Erik the Red, and how his son, Leif the Lucky, had landed in North America long before Christopher Columbus. He bet that Erik had been proud of his Viking son. They had probably been a lot alike.

He and Dad, on the other hand, couldn't be more different.

Kitchen wiped, Sam retreated to his bedroom where he plopped himself on his bed, sighed, and flipped open the book he'd rescued from the basement. *The Saga of the People of Laxardal* wasn't as interesting to him, despite it being about the part of Iceland where Dory had come from, but there was one curious thing. A single word had been scratched in pencil at the top of the chapter: "Saemundur." It looked Icelandic, but it wasn't a word the online translation app recognized. It could be a name. He touched the letters gently, careful not to smudge the graphite.

Who had written it, and why?

CHAPTER TWO

BOLT FROM THE BLUE

"You seriously did what?"

"Don't make me sorry I told you."

"You tell me everything." Derek launched his lanky frame over cracks in the sidewalk with a surprising grace. It was like someone had sprinkled miracle grow over his arms and legs since the start of the summer. Sam hadn't experienced the same growth spurt but expected it would happen any day. "Your dad loves experiments. He was just being weird."

"You're calling someone else weird?" Sam gave him a playful shove, but because Derek was mid-hop, he pinwheeled into the blow-up tube-man in front of Mr. Pendrake's hardware store. As Mr. Pendrake rushed out the front door to rescue his tube-man, Sam rescued a tangled Derek. "Sorry Mr. Pendrake!" he called, and they raced away, laughing.

Derek stopped running first. "I like weird."

"Okay, but this is my dad we're talking about. Mr. Facts and Proof." He shook his head. "Maybe it isn't even real. Is it in my head? Am I imagining it?"

"You do have a very active imagination."

Sam kicked a stone. "The experiment idea was stupid, and it made yesterday stupid." The rest of the summer it would be worse, because Derek was about to leave on vacation with his family.

Sam stopped as they passed Playland, looked up at the neon sign and brightly painted clapboards. "One game of *Turtles*? Dad's running a special for August."

"Can't. Going to the airport as soon as Mom gets back from Julie's."

Julie was Derek's aunt. She lived in Winnipeg and worked at a pet daycare, which made her the perfect person to look after the Mah family's miniature schnauzer, Arnold.

The reality of life without Derek for two weeks settled in. Derek must have felt it too as he frowned and looked at his knees. Holidays were never as much fun when one or the other was away.

"Okay," Sam said. "See ya."

Derek grinned. "Text ya!" And took off in a gangly sprint.

Sam walked through the double front doors of the arcade into joyful chaos.

Playland was one of three interesting things about the village of Gilla Farm. In 1932, Pastor Draven Ezekiel looked at declining membership of his Baptist church and decided what people really needed during hard times of the Great Depression was fun. One day he met a traveller selling a spirometer. The man explained that a spirometer was a gizmo that tested the strength of people's lungs, but instead of a medical machine, this one was made into an arcade game. Pastor Ezekiel was struck by his best idea ever.

He bought the spirometer along with a handful of other interesting machines and opened Playland.

Pastor E ran Playland until 1965, when he died because his heart got too big. The arcade was revived in the 1980s by his great-niece, Penny, who sold it to Sam's dad when they moved to Gilla Farm.

Turtles, an Entex Adventure Vision game that Penny added in the 1980s, was Sam's favourite. He loved the pixelated movements and the *boo-oop* sounds it made.

With a smirk Sam noted he was still reigning champ. He dropped his coin in the slot and assumed his game stance. Shoulders squared and feet planted, he moved his turtle through the simple maze, saving turtlettes from attacking beetles.

If only life were that simple. See a problem, drop a bug bomb. Problem solved.

He had to figure out how to tell Dad what was bugging him. They used to talk about everything. Even the disappearance of his mother hadn't been off limits.

Sam would fix this. He would drop a bug bomb of honesty and clear out the confusion beetles. Today.

He sprinted around the *Law of the West* pinball game, past *Space Invaders* and *Ms. Pac-man*. He stopped short at his father's office door. It was closed, which meant he was either working on paperwork or talking on the phone.

Sam hesitated.

Maybe this wasn't a good time.

The sound of a muffled crash and a "Whoops!" from the office jolted him from his inner wrestling. He spun away.

It was a sign. This talk could wait. Absolutely.

With a stab of shame, Sam left Playland and headed for the park.

Chicken.

He heard a low rumble coming from somewhere beyond the sky's endless blue—the Nordic god Thor was getting ready to swing his magic hammer. No, he had that wrong. Thunder was the sound Thor's magic chariot made as it rolled across the sky. Lightning came from the hammer strike. He shook his head. He was too old to think about myths as if they were real. Like his father, he would think in terms of science and facts. The important thing was that if a storm were moving in, Dad might skip working in his garden. That meant there would be loads of time to talk before dinner. That would work. Sure.

It felt better to tell himself that he wasn't avoiding the conversation. He was making a new plan.

He would begin with a joke, a real one this time, like: "What did the ocean say to the beach?" Answer: "Nothing. It waved."

They would talk as they ate their traditional after dinner bread and peanut butter. One slice with peanut butter spread thick. It was better than ice cream any day of the week except on the days when he and Derek rode their bikes along the Schumann River path and stopped at the Ye Old Soda Shoppe for tiger-tiger ice cream in a cone.

The Schumann River was the second most interesting thing about Gilla Farm. Where it touched the village, it made the shape of a Greek Omega symbol. Dad had told him Omega was a symbol for electrical resistance, but to Sam it just looked like the letter "O" with a bite taken from the bottom. The entire community nestled inside its arc.

The shape was distinctive enough that from space any aliens travelling by would see the river and for sure do a double take.

Sam shielded his eyes from the sun and searched the sky. No aliens, and still no cloud. It was a perfect summer day: sunny with a soft breeze. Except for the distant thunder, Main Street was quiet. Somewhere, kids laughed, a weed-whacker trimmed the edge of a lawn, and a screen door slapped shut. Gilla Farm was too far off the highway to catch the sounds of diesel trucks or other passing traffic, not that they had many visitors.

That was the third most interesting thing about Gilla Farm. You wouldn't find it on a map. Not even the Google car had found it. It wasn't that they were a secret. They were just too small for anyone to care. Inevitably, Gilla Farmites found it easier to tell folks from other places that they lived "just outside Winnipeg."

Gilla Farm was invisible, just like Sam.

He kicked a rock.

The village was laid out like the tail of a peacock. The farther up Main Street you walked, the quieter it got. At the top of Main Street along the arc of the river there was the aptly named Omega Park. To one side of a playground there was a green lamppost, which cast a circle of light for late-night dog-walkers and runners on their way to the river path. All paths led to the river and to a wider path that curved in both directions inside the omega arch and cradled the community. Sam was pretty sure Gilla Farm was the only place you could walk in the opposite direction of your house and still be on your way back home.

He sank to the ground next to the lamppost, sat cross legged, and pulled apart crab grass. Closing his eyes, he tipped his face toward the sun and enjoyed the toasty feeling on his cheeks and forehead. From somewhere beyond the river, he heard the bark of a fox, the wind through leafy treetops, the chittering of squirrels, the buzz of a wasp.

Then everything stopped.

All nature sounds fell away. The wind stilled. Animals and insects quietened.

Sam's eyes fluttered open, and he looked around. That was when he noticed the lamppost. It glowed an icy blue, like something out of a science fiction movie or one of Dad's arcade games. He felt a tingling down his back and noticed the hair on his arms stood straight on end. Weird. He grabbed hold of his feet and curled into a ball to see if he could flex away the tingling.

There was a buzz, a click, then a hissing sound followed by a loud BANG!

He felt as if he were being pulled backward at great speed. As light and the world and awareness faded, he heard something. A woman's voice, her words soft and too far away to make out. They fizzled into nothing, and all went black.

CHAPTER THREE

REVENGE OF THE CUBE PEOPLE

Sam opened his eyes and awkwardly raised himself onto his elbows.

Whoa!

Everywhere he looked there were tiny cubes, as if he were inside a game of *Turtles*. He closed his eyes and shook his head.

Mistake.

His head felt like it might split in two. He groaned, opened his eyes again, and sat all the way up. Slowly, gingerly, he touched his fingertips to his head to make sure it was still in one piece. Had something fallen on him? No bump. Everything ached, even his skin. He ran his palms over the grass, mesmerized by the tiny pink cubes of his hands. The cubes appeared to lag ever so slightly then catch up as he stopped moving. He held a hand in front of his face, waved it back and forth. He felt dizzy.

"Dad," he whimpered, and not just because he was scared. Dad knew brains. He would know what was happening. Colours rushed toward him.

A voice said, "Oh my gosh! Are you hurt?"

That wasn't Dad. He didn't know who it was. All he saw were cubes.

More cubes rushed at him, and more voices:

"Lightning! He was struck by lightning!"

"Impossible. The storm is still miles away!"

"Look at the lamppost, it's gone—"

"Burnt—"

"Exploded—"

"Someone call 911!"

Lightning?

His stomach flipped backward and forward as someone—someones—lifted him onto a bed of moving cubes. Was it a stretcher? It looked like it might be. He cried out, sure he would fall through the loosely connected and shifting stretcher cubes to the ground. But he didn't.

The wooziness was too much. All the colours and cubes began to fade, fade, fade. The last thing he saw was a red glowing light high above him, a shape that wasn't a cube.

It was a jellyfish.

CHAPTER FOUR

MY LIFE AS A SLINKY

After spending Monday and Tuesday night in the hospital, Sam had learned three things:

1. MRI stood for Magnetic Resonance Imaging, and an MRI scan was way louder than a CAT scan, which had nothing to do with cats.
2. His brain, heart, and all the other organs were reading normal. This had Sam's medical team pretty excited.
3. He was no longer invisible to his father, which was funny because it was now difficult for Sam to see him.

His cube-vision had not changed since Monday afternoon in Omega Park. That Sam survived a lightning strike amazed everyone. His shirt had been blown off and there was now a fern-like pattern on his back, as if someone had gotten fancy with a fine-tipped brush and red paint. But he was alive, and hospital staff assured him he would remain that way.

Dad had explained that he'd been hit by a "bolt from the blue" which was a lightning bolt that looked like it was coming from a clear blue sky but was actually from a far-away storm with super-far reach.

A woman on a radio news program said that a bolt from the blue happened in about five percent of lightning strikes, and it was very rare to have one hit a person.

Rare, but still possible.

The news story said that a boy from "just outside Winnipeg" had been struck by such a bolt but would make a full recovery.

He watched as the cubes of his father huddled with the cubes of his doctor next to the cubes of the door. He'd noticed that living cubes had a glow, and more of a 3-D, rounded appearance, while the cubes of objects were 2-D and dull. This had helped him begin to see in a new way. It was still weird, but he was adapting. He fanned his hand back and forth, turning it this way and that. It was like his hand would stretch and resume shape as the cubes followed slightly behind before bouncing back into place. It reminded him of a live-action Slinky toy, like he used to play with as a kid. He'd launched it down the stairs and watched, mesmerized, as the rings stretched and caught up, from one step to the next, repeat, and repeat.

Dad and Dr. Jeremy turned their pink face-cubes his way and moved toward Sam's bed, their mostly connected body cubes slinky-trailing behind them. Dad's hand-cubes picked up Sam's hand cubes. "No internal damage." Dad's voice cracked. "You're going to be fine."

"What about my eyes?" An eye specialist had examined him yesterday.

"Dr. Book said there is no retinal damage, and no burns or abrasions."

"Give it time, Samuel," Dr. Jeremy said. "A lightning strike often affects the nervous system, and vision abnormalities can occur. Thankfully, they are usually temporary."

A waterfall of relief washed over Sam. Then it dried up. "Wait. Usually?"

"We have every reason to believe that as your nervous system recovers from the trauma, your vision will be restored."

Sam swallowed. "But what if it doesn't? What if something is stuck, or something inside my brain is broken?"

Dad squeezed Sam's hand. "Luckily I know a few neurological scientists."

"Should I worry?'

"No, Samuel, not at all. There's a different kind of test we can do than what's available at the hospital. Different equipment."

"Your MRI looks fine," Dr. Jeremy said, "though you are showing significant activity on the left side of your brain, which is fascinating. The test your dad is talking about is called a PET scan."

"I'm guessing it has nothing to do with animals?"

Dr. Jeremy chuckled, and Sam noticed it was getting easier to see the flash of teeth cubes. He could almost see facial expressions. His brain was adapting to this new way of seeing.

"PET is an abbreviation for Positron Emission Tomography," Dad said. "Don't worry about that now. You're going to be fine. This is great news!"

He tried to look happy and excited, but then Dr. Jeremy went on to explain that he would probably have headaches and be super sleepy for a while. He said Sam shouldn't be at all surprised if his body felt like it had been tumbled around in a clothes dryer.

"I feel like that now. My neck hurts, and my back, and my legs and arms." He wiggled his toes. "And the top of my feet!"

"According to our tests the soreness will fade. Before you know it, you'll be right as rain."

Rain! That didn't make him feel better. Where there was rain, sometimes there were storms. Where there were storms, there was lightning. And sometimes lighting came from nowhere.

A pulse began thumping inside Sam's head and he lay back into the pillow.

"Samuel," Dad said, touching his forehead. "Are you okay?"

"Yeah. Just thinking. I mean, could this happen again?"

Dr. Jeremy typed something into his smartphone and read. "The odds of being struck by lightning at all are one in 500,000." He looked back up. "Being struck twice would be very unlikely. I can almost guarantee that it will never again happen to you, or anyone you know."

Sam noticed he said *almost.*

"Okay." His voice was small, but he felt his breath coming back. "When can I go home?"

"That's the other great news," Dad said. "Today! But first we're going to see an old friend."

CHAPTER FIVE

THE RAYNOR INSTITUTE

Sam was grateful for the wheelchair ride out. "Hospital procedure!" the nurse chirped, as if she expected Sam to argue. Why would he? He'd never ridden a wheelchair before. His only argument would have been to drive it himself, but he hadn't yet learned to maneuver his way amongst cubes. That took all his concentration. It was weird and disorienting and he didn't want to bump into anyone.

At the front door, Dad handed him a pair of sunglasses. "I thought dimming the light might help."

The rims and lenses were black, and he was pretty sure they made him look like a secret agent on wheels. The lenses did soften the edges of things, though his vision was still pixelated.

Pixelated! That described his new vision perfectly. It was like he was living inside of one of Playland's old video games.

The doors opened with a hydraulic *whoosh*. The nurse handed over the wheelchair to Dad, and after he bashed the doorframe a few times trying to get the chair to go straight, they were through.

A bolt of icy nerves shot from his head to his toes. His breath came so sudden and fast he had to open his mouth wide to keep up.

"You okay, Samuel?"

Dad sounded far away.

"Samuel? Samuel?"

His father's cubes knelt beside him. The nurse cubes were back, gently pushing his head forward until it was between his knees.

"Breathe, honey," the nurse said. "Just a panic attack."

Calm voices and his father's hand rubbing circles on his back soothed his anxiety. He took deep, steady breathes in and out. "It's just the sky," he finally gasped, "and everything. Very big."

"Completely understandable," the nurse said, but Sam doubted it. How could anyone understand? His doctors had never heard of this thing with his eyes. Blurred vision, sure, even temporary blindness. But not this.

He imagined what he must look like at the top of the ramp with his head bent to his knees. How embarrassing. He took a gulp of air, sat up straight and braced himself.

"You ready?" his father asked.

"I guess."

"Okay, we'll take it slow."

Even more grateful for the wheelchair, he shut his eyes as Dad pushed him to where he'd parked his car. He kept them shut as they drove out of the parking lot. The sunglasses hid his closed eyes, which saved him having to explain. He wasn't sure he could.

The old friend Dad mentioned was at the Raynor Institute, the place he'd worked before they'd moved to

Gilla Farm. During the drive from the hospital, Dad said that he'd made a call and Dr. Engel could fit him in for a PET scan right away. Sam kept his eyes shut behind the sunglasses and tried to listen while his father explained how it would go. The only part Sam really understood was that they would inject him with radioactive stuff which his body would pee out some time later. He wondered if his pee would glow, like the lamppost had just before the lightning strike. Except the glowing pee would be in cubes.

Dr. Engel greeted them warmly and gave Dad one of those double handshakes where he clasped his father's elbow with his free hand. He had wavy blond hair and a wide smile, which made for lots of shiny teeth cubes.

"Good to meet you, Samuel. You're the spitting image of your dad when he was your age."

"You knew him back then?"

"We grew up down the street from each other." Dr. Engel glanced at Dad. "Your dad and I used to terrorize the neighbourhood with pranks."

This was interesting information. Sam looked at his father. "You played pranks?"

"Sort of."

Dr. Engel said, "We had very smart friends, so we took it to another level. Anyone can turn garbage cans upside down. Our pranks required planning, and sometimes weeks to execute."

Dad smiled. "Paul David Hewson."

"Bono!"

"I don't get it," Sam said.

Dr. Engel laughed. "We found out that Bono's real name

was Paul David Hewson. We filled out school registration papers for him, which your dad filed because he worked volunteer hours in the office. We borrowed library books under Paul's name and let them run overdue. What else? Do you remember, Gordie?"

"Not really."

"The classes we'd registered him for were key to the plan. Teachers would mark him absent, because of course he wasn't there, and in the office your dad would erase those absences so that we could keep things going."

"Except I wasn't in the office every day."

"Which made it even better." Dr. Engel was laughing a lot now. "In English class, remember? The secretary called Mr. Sigstad over the intercom and asked if there was a Paul David Hewson in his class. She'd…*haha*, she'd…*haha*, noticed some irregularities in his attendance."

Dad was laughing too. Incredible.

Dr. Engel slapped his knee, and every time he tried to say more, he laughed harder.

"What's so funny?" Sam asked.

"We were probably the only ones who knew the secretary was calling for a superstar. It was a huge joke that only a few people would possibly get."

"What superstar?"

Dr. Engel and Dad stopped laughing.

"Bono?" Dr. Engel said it like it was something Sam should know. "The singer?"

Dad sighed. "Guess we're getting old, Chris. Bono too."

Sam felt like he should apologize. "I don't really listen to old music."

They sighed in unison.

"Your dad was a mastermind. Still is. It's good to see you back here, Gordie."

Dad was silent, and Sam got the feeling he was uncomfortable.

It was like Dr. Engel was talking about a completely different Dad than the one Sam had known his entire life. This other dad was once a kid named *Gordie*. He had friends and played jokes. The Dad Sam knew had always been quiet and serious.

And smart.

Dr. Engel said that they'd played smart pranks and had smart friends which only reminded Sam that Dad didn't want to hang out with him. It was pretty clear that Dad only liked to hang out with smart people.

"Did your father explain the process?" Dr. Engel asked.

"You're going to inject me with something and my pee will glow."

Dr. Engel laughed and slapped his knee again. "There's that same Gordie humour! Good to see some things never change." He chuckled as he made notes on his clipboard. "Sam, your MRI and CAT scans show no sign of lesions on your brain. Today we will look for cell damage along the path the lightning took through your body."

The PET scan machine was like the MRI and CAT machines in that it was a tube he was pushed into while flat on his back. Dr. Engel gave Sam earbuds so that he could listen to the Bono music. He said it would calm and educate him. The doctor needn't have worried. Sam totally got that some people were claustrophobic when stuck in enclosed spaces, but he didn't feel like that. It made him feel safe, far away from open skies and lightning strikes. After a while, he even dozed off.

"You're getting way too comfortable with this," Dad said as they pulled him back out.

Sam rubbed his eyes and stretched. "So now what?"

Before Dad could answer, Dr. Engel was back.

He waved the image in his hand. "You'll want to see this, Gordie."

Dad peered at it. "Yes, hmm, yes."

"Should I be worried?"

Dr. Engel and Dad turned as if they'd just remembered he was there. "No, not at all, Samuel. Dr. Engel was referring to my old area of study."

"Lightning injuries?"

"No, my focus was on how transcranial magnetic stimulation may offer patients who are functionally blind some measure of sight."

"Oh," Sam said. "So let's pretend I have no idea what you're talking about. Am I okay?"

Dr. Engel chuckled before answering. "Absolutely! That, dear boy, is what's fascinating. The scan shows no damage to your cell structure. You are a walking miracle."

"Then what's wrong with my eyes?"

"There are signs that the area of your brain that affects vision may have been stimulated by the electrical currents passing through your body. Your father's old area of study."

"The trans-whatchamacallit."

"Transcranial magnetic stimulation," Dad said. "TMS."

"But that's an aside, Samuel," Dr. Engel said. "All you need to know is that there are no lesions and no scarring. I am confident your sight will return to normal."

"When?"

"Hard to say. Most reported visual abnormalities have involved hallucinations and flashes of light. Any of those?"

Sam remembered the weird light, the last thing he saw before waking up in the ambulance. "There was something. Just before I passed out, I saw a red blob in the sky. It looked like a jellyfish."

Dr. Engel made a note on his clipboard. "We may attribute that to the trauma of your injury. Anything since then?"

"Nope."

"Give it time. I have every reason to believe that as the swelling caused by the stimulation goes down, your vision will be restored."

"Until then," Dad said, "I want to know everything. Any changes, even the smallest thing. Okay?" There was a vibration coming from his father, like small waves of excitement.

"You're going to study me?"

"No, of course not. I'm going to monitor you."

"Maybe you should," Dr. Engel said. "Study his progress, make a few notes. Open up your old files. You still have them?"

"I do."

"Your son's injury, as terrible and frightening as it may have been, could offer valuable insight."

Insight. Sam smiled at the word. In a way, seeing pixels was like looking inside of what was there. A little. *In* sight.

More vibration. Dad turned back to Sam. "How would you feel about that, Samuel?"

"I…I don't know. Could it help blind people?"

"Functionally blind," he corrected. "That means their eyes function, but not enough to get by as a sighted person. I don't know if it will help, but I wouldn't mind pulling out some of my old work, looking into it."

What a switcheroo! Last week Sam had studied his father. Now it was his turn to be his father's experiment.

Dr. Engel had those wide smile cubes again, while Dad just softly vibrated.

It would mean they would hang out. Not quite the way Sam had planned, but it was something.

"Okay. Maybe you can show me the right way to do a scientific process, or whatever." Just like he had with Thyla.

"Deal," his father said.

Big shiny grins all around. Even Dad.

CHAPTER SIX

PEANUT BUTTER AND PUZZLES

Leaving the Institute was just as difficult as leaving the hospital, except this time he knew to take deep breaths and keep his eyes shut behind the sunglasses. A half hour later they were home and having lunch.

"Dr. Engel made you sound like someone different."

Eyebrow vees. "How do you mean?"

"No offence, Dad, but you're not exactly the 'jokester' he remembers. Not that I've seen." Sam used air quotes for "jokester" as if it weren't a real word, even though he knew it was.

Corner mouth-cubes up—a smile. "You're right, Samuel. Time has a way of changing a person."

"I can't imagine you doing the 'Gordie'"—he used air quotes again—"pranks Dr. Engel talked about. They did sound funny. Maybe I should try some."

Another smile. "You be you, Samuel. You've got plenty of spirit all your own."

Sam smiled. *Spirit* wasn't *smarts*, but it had the same number of letters, and it wasn't nothing.

"Am I more like you were at my age, or like Dory?"

Sam saw Dad's shoulders droop a little, like all the smile went out of him. Talking about Dory never used to make Dad sad. Nothing had. He'd always been serious, but not sad. When had it begun? Not as long as a year ago, because that summer had been perfect. They'd gone to the beach and ridden their bikes and when Dad looked at him it was with his eyes connected to his brain and he was all the way there. Not somewhere else.

It wasn't at his grade six parent-teacher conference last fall. Even when he found out Sam was struggling in math, Dad squeezed his shoulder, smiled, and told him not to worry. He said it would come.

It might have been just before last Christmas—at his twelfth birthday. He'd thought then that Dad was embarrassed because the cake he'd baked was gummy on the inside and the icing was runny. Sam hadn't cared. It was sweet and gooey and delicious, but when Dad left the table, he sat on the couch and stared at a spot on the wall beside the TV instead of looking at the evening news.

That was it. Sam was sure of it. Dad's sadness, and the distance, began at his last birthday. But why?

Dad reached over and ruffled Sam's hair. "There are parts of you like Dory and parts like me, but most of all you are someone completely new. You're Samuel Templeton." He did not use air quotes.

Sam wondered if things would have been different if Dory had stuck around, if Dad would have been a guy who laughed and kept playing pranks.

"Did Dory ever talk about when she was a kid?"

"Sure. Sometimes. You already know most of it."

"Not really."

Dad leaned closer. "Are you finding it hard to remember things, Samuel?"

"No, nothing like that," he said. "I mean, I know she's from Iceland and that she lived with her uncle, but those are the *facts*." He remembered that Dad liked facts. "And that's great, but what was she like when she was my age? Did she have friends? Did she play baseball and soccer? Did she have a favourite book? Did she play jokes like you and Dr. Engel did?"

Dad sighed and shook his head pixels. "I'm sorry. I don't know."

Sam sighed too. Maybe when his eyes got better, he would make some stuff up and write it in a journal, sort of build a story of her life with the tiny bits he knew. He sighed again.

But Dad wasn't finished. "She didn't talk about her daily life growing up. It wasn't until after she left that I realized how often she would change the subject from her past." He frowned. "I wondered then if she'd been hiding something. No, that's unfair." He considered. "It felt more like she'd decided to leave something behind."

"What?"

He sighed and shrugged. "Probably the same as every young person who wants to carve their own way. Your mother was a strong person. When she made her mind up about something, that was it."

Except, Sam thought, *she'd changed her mind about Iceland.* She returned to the country of her birth and left him and Dad behind.

Dad had told him how Dory had sent one single letter. She said she wouldn't write again and was true to her word.

It hadn't mattered so much when he was too young to understand, but as he got older he wondered about all kinds of things, including why she left. Of *course* he wondered if she didn't love him, and if her leaving was his fault. What kid wouldn't?

Dad assured Sam that she loved him very much. He said that some people felt the pull for home so strongly that it was bigger than the whole world. He also said that he and Dory were young when they married, and that she had to go home to finish growing up.

It wasn't a perfect answer, but it was okay. Dad made sure it was okay.

In between bites of peanut butter, mayo and lettuce sandwiches, he tilted his head this way and that, playing with his new vision in his old kitchen while Dad explained how the week would go. It mostly involved his staying home from the arcade to babysit Sam. He didn't say "babysit" but that's what it was. Everything that used to be easy was now more difficult. It was frustrating.

He thought about how when he played a new video game it was always hard at first. With practice it got easier. The fact of the pixels was actually pretty cool. He just needed practice.

"You don't need to stay home. I can't ride my bike or anything like that, but I can do some stuff like I used to."

"Of course you can, Samuel. I'll stick around for a few days just to see how it goes. Okay?"

Sam nodded.

"And try not to worry. Remember what Dr. Jeremy said. Don't be surprised if you wake up tomorrow and everything is back to normal."

Sam mashed bread and lettuce between his molars, savouring the mix of salty mayo with sweet peanut butter. His father bit into his sandwich too. They sat, chomping and staring at each other. After two whole days together, he had his father's attention—just what he'd hoped for. But there was something missing.

Sam remembered how his father's cubes looked when he spoke with Dr. Engel. There'd been a shininess to them. What was that? Interest? Excitement? Whatever it was, he didn't have it now.

"Dad, why did you stop working at the Institute?"

Dad took another bite of sandwich, swallowed, and took a gulp of milk before answering. "It's complicated."

"As complicated as my eyes?"

"I wanted a change after your mother left. Thought it would help."

"Did it?"

"I love our life here, Samuel. I think you do too." Eyebrows up. "Do you?"

"Sure! I mean, I don't know anything else, but this is good."

Dad shrank back in on himself. Sam didn't need clear vision to see his father's attention begin to shift and go somewhere far away. He could sense it.

"Why Gilla Farm?"

Dad came back from wherever he'd been drifting. "What do you mean?"

"Almost no one knows about Gilla Farm. We could have moved anywhere. Why did we move here?"

Dad finished his sandwich, dabbed at his mouth with a paper napkin and then folded the napkin upon his plate.

Sam saw all of this, and also his father's unhappiness. The pixels made Sam look harder, which meant that he was actually seeing more.

For instance, when Dad lifted his eyebrows and pushed up his bottom lip, he was about to ask a question. If he didn't ask, that meant he still had a question, but was keeping it on the inside.

When Dad's eyes opened really wide with both brows lifted and pulled together in the middle, that meant he was scared. He had done a lot of that when they were in the ambulance.

Right now, his eyebrows were lifted just a little, and corners of his lips were pulled down. He was definitely sad.

"Before you were born, your mother and I would take drives in the country. One day we came across a tree-lined side road off the highway and wondered where it would take us. This village was a lovely surprise. After we discovered the ice-cream shop, that was it. We came back every weekend until you were born."

Now he looked even more sad.

"I didn't really think too hard about it," he continued. "I remembered seeing a for sale sign in the window of Playland and thought it would be a good change."

Sam loved Gilla Farm, and so did Dad, despite his sadness. Maybe he missed his being a research scientist.

"Why don't you dig out your old work? The stuff Dr. Engel talked about."

Dad pulled a hand through his hair. "It's been boxed up for a long time. I'm not sure if my computer files will even work anymore. They were made on a pretty old system."

"You're the smartest person I know. You'll figure it out."

Dad's eye-cubes crinkled in a happy sort of way, even if he didn't all-out smile. "Okay. I'll start tomorrow morning."

Sam picked up the plates. "I got this, Dad. And you have a whole afternoon to work in your garden."

"You sure?"

"Sure! Like I said. I can still do stuff."

As Sam rinsed their plates and put them in the dishwasher, he waved his hands back and forth in front of his face. It didn't make him woozy anymore. He even kind of liked how one cube followed the next in perfect synchronicity.

He moved about the kitchen swaying and waving. Imagining what he must look like made him giggle and feel better than he had in three days. He danced himself out of the kitchen, touched the flat pixels of the doorframe and ran his palms along the pixels of the walls. In the living room there were colours, colours everywhere. It was beautiful. A new way of seeing.

Overwhelmed with a wish to jump amongst the tall grasses in the ditch, he whirled himself toward the front door, flung the door open, leapt over the two steps and onto his front lawn.

Where his stomach dropped.

Just like at the hospital, ice shot through his body and exploded every nerve.

He was terrified.

CHAPTER SEVEN

FARADAY, FARADONE

Sam fell to his knees, the afternoon sun like a knife through his head.

It was a panic attack, same as at the hospital. He breathed deep, heard the nurse's voice in his head, told himself he could handle this—just like he could make peanut butter sandwiches and do the dishes.

Maybe not quite like that.

He imagined his father rubbing his back.

Breathe, Samuel, breathe. Come on, you know how this works.

He did. One-two-three-four in, one-two-three-four out. Repeat. Repeat.

His pulse slowed a little, enough for his brain to work better. He didn't think he could stand up, so with his eyes shut tight, he crawled hand over hand until he reached his front step. Then up, and up, and back inside the house.

Finally, sitting with his knees to his chest and leaning against the inside of the front door, he opened his eyes. His heart thumped over the unfairness of everything that had happened since he'd been hit by that stupid bolt of lightning. His stomach buzzed like it was full of hornets until one vibrated an idea up to his brain.

Whoa.

Sam knew what had caused his panic attacks.

It was lightning and knowing that it could strike him even when the sky was clear. Every fibre of his being was sending him a big NOPE! to going outdoors.

He shook his head. Staying inside for the rest of his life wasn't going to work for him.

Hey, brain, the chance of it happening again is one in 500,000.

Hey, Sam, his brain argued, *one in 500,000 is still a chance.*

It was like that saying about how once you know something you can't unknow it. Was that a saying? Sam was pretty sure it was.

He took more deep breaths. One-two-three-four in. One-two-three-four out. Sam wasn't sure where he'd heard about the deep breathing thing. It might have been at school, or maybe from Derek, the king of facts. Derek loved books with titles like *The Abridged Book of Every Known Fact in the World. Abridged* meant shortened, which meant that Derek knew a short something about everything.

He wished Derek were here now. They'd texted while Sam was in the hospital. That was when he'd discovered, weirdly, that he could see stuff on his screen perfectly clear and normal. Tapping on the keyboard image on his phone was easy, but he couldn't read words written on paper. On paper, the pixels made everything inside each cube fuzzed together.

He'd texted his pal about the lightning and his vision. Derek responded in a perfectly Derek way.

Derek: *1st. Glad u r not ded*
Sam: *Me too*
Derek: *2nd. It sounds supr cool*
Sam: *Hows Quebec?*
Derek: *Very French. I'll bring you a baguette.*

Having a buzzing ball of hornets in his belly was not cool. It made him feel trapped.

Outside there was baseball and soccer and fishing and riding his bike. And what about school? Besides class, friends were there, and games, and all kinds of stuff.

Staying inside for the rest of his life was not an option.

He would think like his father: sensible and rational. What was happening wasn't that different from a scary movie. It was only scary because you didn't know what would happen next. Ergo, if Sam learned everything about lightning, the panic attacks would go away.

He trotted between hallway wall pixels to his room. His laptop was on his desk, blank screen cubes at the ready. He fumbled around for the power button and pressed. The screen turned crystal clear, but there was another problem. He couldn't see his keyboard. Why could he see what was on the screens of his laptop and phone clearly, while everything in real life was in pixels?

Derek might know. Sam woke up his phone. When the virtual keyboard popped up, he texted.

Derek: *That's prob cause screed pixels and world pixels are the same size. Don't ask.*
Sam: *Screed? Just kidding typo king but I can't see my keyboard to Google stuff*

Derek: *Use your mic dufus. Or stick with phone. Got 2 go. Dinner. Tonight we are sleeping in a submarine.*
Sam: *So cool and thanks*

Sam couldn't remember where the mic button was on his keyboard, or even if it was there at all, but he could clearly see the small virtual helper icon floating in the top right corner of his screen. He used his touch pad and clicked on it. "Tell me about lightning," he said. The search engine returned almost five hundred million results.

Pretty soon his head was crammed with information about positive and negative charges, ice crystals, and 'bolts from the blue.'

He already knew that was what hit him. He needed to know more.

A bolt from the blue was lightning that shot upward through a storm cloud and out the leading lip on top called the *anvil*—which was cool because that is exactly what it looked like. The bolt could go for miles before a ground strike, which made it look like it was coming out of a clear blue sky. It was rare.

One in 500,000 is still a chance, Sam.

Be quiet, brain!

On a very long page of information, Sam learned there were many kinds of lightning besides bolts from the blue, like spider lightning and dry lightning. He liked the related stuff about ancient gods and myths, which he already knew a whole lot about from reading so many books about Norse mythology—like how Thor was the god of thunder and lightning.

He learned too that there were scientific phenomena called sprites and elves, which had nothing to do with myths. An elf was a kind of radio wave, and the letters stood for Extra Low Frequency. A sprite was a gigantic electrical discharge high above a storm cloud. He clicked on the sprite link and came to an image that looked a lot like a jellyfish.

It was what he'd seen in the sky just before he'd blacked out in Omega Park! It wasn't exactly like that, but sort of.

He followed one link after another until he landed on something so interesting and so perfect he felt positively charged.

In 1836 a British scientist named Michael Faraday invented a cage that could protect machines and people from lightning strikes.

His brain rapid-fired. If he had a cage he could go outdoors. Except a cage didn't move. But what if it could?

There were lots of do-it-yourself projects on the internet. He would find instructions for how to put wheels on a cage. Even better, what if he found a way to make a Faraday cage he could wear like a suit?

He searched and found a video of a guy wearing chain mail doing something with an umbrella and electrical bolts. It was cool, but not the how-to Sam needed. He had no idea how to make or get chain mail.

Another video showed a power line worker who called his work clothes a "hot suit." It was also called a conductive suit. He said that the metal thread made it act like a Faraday cage.

That was it!

Thyla's mom was a power line technician. If Mrs. Smith could help him get a hot suit, then he wouldn't have to build a walking cage.

Sam burst into the kitchen just as his father set plates for supper on the table.

"Hey, buddy, slow down! Unless?" His face showed hopeful signs, then flattened as Sam shook his head.

As his father filled the table with his favourite comfort foods—grilled peanut butter and cheese sandwiches, fresh sliced cucumbers in sour cream, and tomato soup—Sam told him about what he'd learned.

Dad looked confused. "This is all very interesting, Samuel, but why exactly do you want one of Mrs. Smith's hydro suits?"

Sam took a breath. "When I tried to go outside, I couldn't." He felt his face crumple. "This is so dumb. I don't know why I'm like this."

"Like what, Samuel?" As his father sat down, he bumped his knee against the table leg, which made the table jump.

Sam automatically shot out his hand to steady the soup pot. "I can't help it. I can't make it stop. It's like my whole body won't let me go outside. I know it's because of the lightning."

There was only a brief look of surprise pixels from his dad. He squeezed Sam's shoulder, urged him to continue.

"It doesn't matter that there's a one in 500,000 chance I'll get hit again. My brain doesn't care."

His father waited through all of Sam's starts and stops and a final deep breath before he spoke. "Anxiety is like that, Samuel. It's not something you can reason away. Not really. What you're doing now? The deep breaths? That's a good idea."

"I don't want to be afraid."

"I know. You think that wearing one of Mrs. Smith's suits will help?"

"Maybe."

His father squished his brows together as he ladled soup into Sam's bowl. "Are you sure you want to do this, Sam? Walking around in a suit like that might—" He sighed. "Sometimes other kids can be unkind."

"Believe me, I know," he said too quickly.

"I'm sorry to hear that, son."

"No, I don't mean it's a problem or anything. It's just that I see it, you know? I *am* in the world."

Dad's forehead pixels smoothed.

"I have to do something to get myself outside or I will feel like this thing inside me, this anxiety—" It was Sam's turn to squish his brows. "What if it changes me? Like forever? Even if my eyes do get back to normal?"

"When." His father's voice was gentle. "Don't say *if.* Your eyes will get back to normal, Samuel. This is only temporary. Remember that."

"But what about the being scared part? What if that part never gets back to normal? I feel like my brain is split in two, and the thinking part has to prove to the scared part that I can do this. That's why I have to get outside."

His father nodded. "Okay. After dinner, I'll go see the Smiths. No promises, but it won't hurt to ask."

For the first time since his accident Sam felt like everything would work out. He took big crunchy bites of his sandwich with spoonfuls of soup and mashed everything up in his mouth. When his belly was finally filled, it was like there was no space left for fear.

Dad pulled on his shoes. "I'll be right back."

"I'll do the dishes," Sam said. It didn't take long: one frying pan, one soup pot, two plates and bowls and spoons.

Dad wasn't a fancy cook, but Sam didn't mind. Sometimes when he ate at Derek's, Mrs. Mah would make things like ricotta cannelloni if it was Italian night, or beyenatu if it was Ethiopian night. Derek's mom was a lunchtime chef at a fancy hotel in the city. You'd think a chef would be pretty sick of cooking when they were at home. Not Mrs. Mah.

He wondered if Dory had liked to cook. Even though Dad did his best to make things okay, it did bother him that somewhere in the world he had a mother that had walked away from him like he didn't even exist. The *idea* of it bothered him. You couldn't actually miss someone you never knew. Or could you?

Mrs. Mah never had an Icelandic night. Sam was pretty sure that was intentional. She probably thought thinking about Iceland would make him sad about Dory, which wasn't at all true. But she was doing a nice thing, and he didn't want to be rude. He would love to taste what they ate in Iceland. Except for the legends, all he knew about his mother's country was that it had volcanoes and lots of sheep and fish. Even though it was too cold to grow peanuts, they probably still ate peanut butter. Almost everyone who wasn't allergic to it loved peanut butter. It was practically a law of the universe.

The kitchen door opened, and his father walked in with Mrs. Smith's hot suit.

"She said she was happy to help." He draped the hot suit over the back of a chair. It was a little big, but they could adjust it with duct tape and pins.

"Too bad I don't have virtual goggles that would let me see things clearly, like when I look at a computer screen. I could strap them on like Thyla's birdwatching goggles."

"Who?" Dad's brow pixels were lifted. It didn't look like he was joking.

"Thyla. Thyla Smith? From next door?"

Dad's eye pixels squinched and his brows now smashed in the middle. "Mr. and Mrs. Smith are our neighbours."

"Thyla, Dad. Thyla! Their daughter. The whiz brain you tutored and who everyone likes." He clamped his lips shut before he blurted out his jealousy. Why was Dad pretending he didn't know her?

His father took him gently by the shoulders. "I think we should go back to the hospital."

CHAPTER EIGHT

SPACEMAN SAM

Thyla was missing.

Why was he the only one who knew this? The terrible dream that began Monday afternoon was getting worse.

In the morning, Dad insisted on a visit to Dr. Jeremy, who said he checked out fine, but Dad wouldn't let them leave the hospital until Sam fibbed that he'd fallen asleep on the couch and must have woken up mixed-up with a dream. He couldn't think of any other way.

He *knew* Thyla was real. Now he had even more reason to get back out in the world. Someone else had to remember her.

"Lift up your arms, Samuel." After measuring Sam's torso, legs, and waist, his father used duct tape to fold in and tuck away the extra few inches of fabric in Mrs. Smith's suit.

As Dad taped, Sam thought some more about the mystery of Thyla. He would use the Nine Step Scientific Method to figure it out.

First the question. It wasn't "Does Thyla exist?" He knew she did. The real question was why his father and her parents didn't know the same thing.

To formulate his hypothesis, he would first go out and

talk to other people from Gilla Farm. He'd worry about the next step in the scientific method when he came to it.

Guilt washed through him as he remembered that just a few days ago he'd wished Thyla would go away. He'd also wished for his father's attention. Both wishes came true, but not in a way he wanted. Not at all.

"There you go, Sam." Dad finished his duct tape alterations. "Why don't you give it a test?"

He looked in the full-length mirror on the back of the bathroom door. His brain had adapted to his pixelated vision, and what he saw looked amazing! It was a suit straight out of Tony Stark's laboratory in the Marvel comic universe. He pulled the silvery hood over his head, completing the image.

"This is perfect, thanks!"

Dad smiled gently. "You look like a spaceman."

Sam thought so too. To his father he said, "This suit is a scientific marvel." Did he see approval in his father's eyes?

"Are you sure you want to do this, Sam? It is easy to say you can handle unkind comments, but words can really hurt."

"I know."

Dad put a hand on his shoulder. "Promise me you will talk to me if something happens. I want to know if anything or anyone is bothering you." He had his serious look. Or, extra serious, because serious was his normal.

Sam gulped. "I promise, Dad. I will tell you everything. For your scientific study."

"I don't mean for the study."

Sam wanted to say that Dad could talk about his stuff too. Instead, he pulled on his rubber-soled sneakers, and with his best salute, made his way to the front door.

It was time to go outside.

He turned the door handle and let the door swing wide.

No buzzing ball in his gut, but there were flutters. More like butterflies than hornets. Butterflies he could handle.

He braced himself and took one big step.

More flutters. Nothing worse. He licked his lips and shuffled onto the front walk, turned and gave Dad a thumbs up. “I’ll be home by supper.”

A small surge of joy pulsed through him. He tried one hop-step, then another. He was still anxious, but as long as he was wearing this suit, he would be okay. He’d found his own solution. Him! Not Dad, and not the doctor. Sam Templeton. Maybe he was smart in his own way, a different kind of smart than Dad. A different kind of smart than Thyla.

He was eager to talk to other people in Gilla Farm. They would probably tell him Thyla moved into a dorm in the city. But why wouldn’t his dad or her parents know that?

As he walked toward Main Street, the belly butterflies moved with him. He breathed in-two- three, and out-two-three. He could do this.

Sam imagined the butterflies, all yellow, green, and blue in magnificent, cubed patterns flying up from his gut and out the top of his head, joining other buzzing and fluttering insects in picking up pollen and sharing it from flower to flower. The world was beautiful! Living cubes moved and breathed and swelled with extra shine against the flat, dull, non-living cubes. Smells were different too, sharper: roses, pine, fresh cut grass.

A car burning oil.

Bro-o-oom!

It was Randy and his vintage car. The baby blue 1973 Vauxhall Viva was practically an antique, at least as old as Sam's dad. Randy bought it when he'd turned sixteen last March. When he wasn't working part time at the gas station, he was fixing his car, restoring it, taking it out for test drives, and then pushing it back home after it inevitably conked out. Randy stuck his arm out the wide-open window and waved. "Hey, Sam, that you?"

Sam nodded and widened the hood to show more of his face.

"Thought so. I heard about the suit. Good to see you!"

News travelled fast. "You too! Car sounds good."

A teeth flash and he was gone before Sam had a chance to ask about Thyla.

Rats. Next time.

Sam walked past his school where a couple of kids were tossing a baseball. He could tell who they were by body movement and his growing adjustment to his new sight. There was Filipe Yanez whose family had emigrated from Chile last year. Filipe played piano—classical on account of the lessons he took with Mr. Budoloski—but he wanted to be a rock star. He was sure he'd be in a band by the time they hit high school.

Filipe threw the ball to Teresa Field, who believed the world would be saved through volunteer work. She and her family had spent July in Kenya building a school for an organization called Hope Story.

They must have spotted him, because Filipe called "Hey!" and he and Teresa trotted over.

"That you, Sam?" Teresa asked.

"Does *everyone* know I'm wearing this suit?"

Filipe shrugged. "I heard it from Danielle who heard it from Sherri who heard it from Lori."

"I heard it from Cheryl," Teresa said, "who heard it from Tracey who heard it from Val who heard it from Lori. Lori heard it from her mom. Someone must have been talking about it at her store."

"Probably my dad," Sam said. "We ran out of peanut butter."

Teresa mocked shock. "I can't believe you let that happen!"

Sam grinned. "Guess I was distracted."

"Seriously, man, you okay?" Filipe's face pixels looked worried.

"I can't see very well, but that's only temporary."

Teresa tilted her head. "So why the suit? We only heard you were wearing it. Not why. Is it some sort of extra protection?"

"It's lame," Sam said, "but I'm freaked out by lighting. My brain knows it probably won't happen again, but if it does this hot suit will keep me from getting shocked."

Filipe leaned in and put his hand on his shoulder. "Anxiety, man. I get it. Don't worry about it."

Teresa nodded. "Whatever it takes. We all get it."

It was so nice to hear that Sam began to feel emotional. He coughed it away before things got awkward. "I have a question for you guys."

"Shoot," Filipe said.

"When was the last time you saw Thyla?"

Two face scrunches.

"Is that on Showflix?" Teresa asked.

Sam tried again. "Thyla who went to our school. Graduated early…going to U of M. Ring a bell?"

Two shaking heads.

"You sure?" Teresa asked.

Filipe leaned in again, peered at him.

Sam smiled weakly. "Must be one of those deep dreams I had right after the accident."

Filipe slapped him on the back. "Time to wake up, man! And get better soon, okay? We should hang out!"

"How about now?" Teresa asked.

Sam grinned. "Thanks, but I think my eyes are too wonky for ball."

"You can still hang out," Filipe said.

"I have something I need to do. Have fun."

"You too, man!"

As his friends trotted back to the schoolyard, Sam felt great tidal waves of gratitude. If his eyes never healed his friends would still hang out, even if he was wearing this suit.

Still anxious, but not as much, he turned up Main Street, walked past Playland and Ye Old Soda Shoppe. He kept going until he reached Omega Park.

Other than a charred circle there was no sign there had ever been a lamppost. The ground where it used to be told its own story. A beautiful one. Even cubed he could see it was like an artist had taken a paintbrush to it and made a feathery, fern-like pattern in the clipped green grass. It reminded Sam of the red pattern on his back.

Sam bent and traced along the impression with his gloved hand. It was easy to see because the living grass cubes were shiny and full compared to the flat of the pattern.

It wasn't burnt. It was pale, as if someone had dribbled chemical paint cleaner along it.

This was the scene of the crime, so to speak. He checked his nerves. So far, so good—no belly buzzing, and his pulse was even. He took off a glove, turned his pink hand pixels this way and that.

No anxiety. Just sunlight and warmth. After a steadying breath, he moved his hands to his hood, pushed it back—

"Nope-nope-nope!"

He was nearly knocked over by a wave of dizziness. He put the hood back in place and breathed.

Okay, so no glove was okay. No hood was not okay. Baby steps. He spread his fingers wide and pressed against the pale pattern.

This time he was knocked back, and more. It felt like he was both in the park and in a tunnel being sucked backward. He broke into a sweat and his breath came hard and fast as light swirled around him. He felt pins and needles run up and down his back and heard himself talking.

No, it wasn't his voice. With a start he realized it was the same voice and words he'd heard when he'd been struck by lightning. A woman's voice.

Everything you need is inside of you.

The phrase repeated over and over in his head as the tunnel of lights swirled away and he found himself exactly where he should be, where he'd been all along. He was in the park, his bare hand against the pattern in the grass. He sat back.

That was weird.

It must have been another kind of panic attack brought on by his return to the exact place where all this began. The phrase was probably just something he'd read somewhere. *Everything you need is inside of you.* It was a good message, which is probably why it got stuck in his head.

Deep breath in, deep breath out. That he could remove the glove with no issues was a very good sign. Today the glove, tomorrow—or the next day—the hood. It meant that the panic attacks, like his wonky vision, were temporary. He took both gloves off and stuck them in his pockets.

On the other side of the clearing, there was a playpark. Two moms and a dad watched their squealing children climb on a slide made to look like a giant wooden ship. Not far from the playpark, a girl threw a frisbee for a huge black and tan dog.

Sam recognized the dog as Finny, a Bernese Mountain Dog, which meant the girl was Manju Khandelwal. There was only one Bernese Mountain Dog in Gilla Farm and she belonged to Manju.

The pattern was too interesting to ignore. Sam walked along each branch as if balanced on a tightrope high above the ground.

Then he saw the trench.

It was two-inches deep and ran in a straight line from where the lamppost used to be toward the trees that lined the river. He followed the trench and noticed that along its length the weeds had been overturned. There were clumps of soil kicked to the side, as if someone had taken a garden hoe to it. He followed to where it curved left into the trees at the edge of the clearing. He continued to follow until the trench disappeared into the clay of the river path.

So much for that.

He heard a sound, out of place amongst bird twitters and the burble of the river. A strange bird, or maybe a squirrel. It almost sounded like crying. He decided to take a chance and push the fabric of his hood away from one ear. All okay—no panic.

He listened.

It *was* crying! It was soft and coming from somewhere above. He looked up into the forest canopy and nearly fainted.

A squat creature perched on a branch. It was a robin egg blue colour, with chubby cheeks and a bulbous nose, no hair except for a pair of bright yellow eyebrows.

It wasn't pixelated.

"Hallo?" it said.

CHAPTER NINE

FLUM

"Hallo, hallo, hallo? Can you help me?" the creature pleaded. Its voice rose and tumbled like rivulets of water over stone.

Were hallucinations another kind of panic attack?

Sam rubbed his eyes. "Not possible," he told the air.

"Oh," the creature said, its shiny head slumped over its narrow chest.

Sam blinked at it. "I just—" His mind went blank.

The creature looked at him again. Hope widened its eyes.

Sam checked his breathing, patted his belly for buzzing hornets. Nothing. This did not feel like a panic attack. He did not feel panic. Surprise and disbelief, yes, but not panic. He opened his mouth to speak. But what to say? The creature watched him as he made "muh-muh-muh-muh" sounds under his breath.

This…thing, whatever it was, could not exist.

Could it?

The leaves it sat on and against were bent from its weight, and it was as if Sam could hear the breeze adjust its path and move around the creature before it whispered on its way.

Sam pinched himself.

"Ow!"

Concern flooded the creature's eyes.

It did exist.

Sam gulped.

With its broad bottom and narrow shoulders, the creature's torso looked like a teardrop falling from a large head. Its legs were short and its feet long. Its arms ran nearly its whole length. Against its blue skin, its clothing was silver as minnows in moonlight—like Sam's suit, but a much better fit. Slung over its head and shoulders, there was a green satchel very like the book bag Dad had given Sam last Christmas.

Sam jumped back as the creature slid from the tree and speed-wobbled toward him.

"Yikes!" he cried.

The creature froze, then tilted its head. "I'm not going to hurt you."

Sam shut his eyes so tight it made him dizzy. When he opened them again the creature was on tippy toes in front of him, attempting a closer look at Sam's face.

Sam stood five foot even and the monster only came up to his waist. A two-foot-high monster wasn't terribly frightening, no matter how strange.

This week had been bizarre right out of the gate.

The fear it might attack him melted away. The fear that he'd lost his mind remained.

The creature thrust a plump left thumb toward Sam's hand and wiggled it. "I am Flum," it announced. "May all be very well."

It wiggled its thumb again and raised two bushy, yellow brows as if waiting on Sam to make the next move.

Perplexed, Sam lifted his thumb and immediately found it hooked in a thumb-shake. Once up, once down.

Perhaps the most startling thing was that Sam could see it clearly, as if the lightning strike and his garbled vision hadn't happened—except that the trees, the path, even his own hand, were all still in pixels.

So that was weird.

"Nice, ah, to meet you, but—" he looked around. There was no one on the path, no one to share this weirdness.

Flum looked serious. "Please, I need your help."

It helicoptered its arms all around, reminding Sam of Mr. Pendrake's tube-man, and Derek.

"I have asked and pleaded and begged someones to help me, but no one will and I'm scared!" It began sobbing again.

Sam searched his pockets, but he wasn't in the habit of carrying tissues. Hesitantly, he reached over and patted Flum's shoulder. "There, there," he said. Flum grasped hold of his arm and cried on it as if it were a towel.

Finally, tears spent, its face split in two with a grin that stretched from ear to ear. "Thank you, oh, thank you. I have felt so alone."

Despite the weird factor, Sam felt his heart ache for the poor creature.

Flum breathed in deep and let out a heavy sigh, then hopped up on a bench at the side of the path. It patted the space beside it and Sam sat too.

"This will sound rude," Sam said, "but what are you?"

"Not rude, not at all. After three nightfalls I have seen no other self like me. I am from Osborne." It held up a chubby palm. Sam wasn't sure if it was a wave or a salute.

"Osborne is a different elsewhere. But this place, this *here*, is not on any map I've seen. If I don't know about you, you don't know about Osborne. Unless...do you?" Its eyes brightened.

"No."

It sighed then said, "My turn. Who are you, and where am I?" The creature sat still as stone as it waited for an answer.

"I'm Sam, I guess."

"Sam-I-Guess?"

"I am. I am Sam." He stifled a giggle, which was more about nerves than humour. "This planet is Earth. Is Osborne another planet?"

"No," it wailed. "I mean, yes, but more. It is an alternate."

"An alternate what?"

That stopped Flum. "You don't know about alternates?"

Uncertain, Sam shook his head. "Maybe not?" Sam knew the meaning of the word per his dictionary, but suspected this creature meant something else.

It looked solemn. "We have much to share." It plopped itself in the dirt, reached for a stick, and scratched a long line. "Once, there was one path." It drew a circle on the line. "When the first world began its great journey, it came to shift-points where its path would fork. Rather than going one way, or the other, it went both, each existing simultaneously." It scratched two more lines from the circle. "As these paths forked again and again, the same thing happened. Over time the worlds came to stop and began to evolve and change in the spaces they settled. Thus"—it slapped its chest—"Osbornian and"—it slapped Sam's chest—"Earthian."

Sam looked warily at Flum. "We say, 'Earthling.' How come I haven't heard of planet alternates? There are really strong telescopes that would have discovered them."

"They are not to be seen by telescopes. They exist in another time and place, the same as here but different. The only way to reach alternates is through"—their bottom lip quivered—"magical shifts."

"There's no such thing as magic."

Flum looked at Sam as if he'd suddenly grown a third head.

Sam closed his eyes hard, and then opened them. Flum was still there. Maybe he shouldn't debate the existence of magic with a creature from another world. "Are you saying that my planet is like a different version of yours?"

"Yes! Some planets are just planets, but alternates are more. They are changed by the path. Still a planet but connected."

"And a…shift…is a doorway between alternates?"

It began sobbing again. "Yes! But it's gone!"

Once again, Sam patted the creature on its shoulder. After a moment, it took a calming breath and quieted.

"You said you've been here three, um…nightfalls. That means you got here on Monday. Today is Thursday," he said, and added, "Those are names we have for days of the week so we don't get mixed up."

Flum nodded. "Moon's Day and Thor's Day. We have the same."

"Thor? Like the ancient Norse god?"

"They are the same."

The creature's way of speaking was odd, as if it was used to a different language but still understood English very well.

"On Monday, I had an accident," Sam pointed through the trees. "Just over there. I was struck by lightning. It changed my eyes, and now I see things mixed up. That's why when I saw you, I thought you weren't real."

"I am real."

Sam took a breath, "It's a lot to believe. Stuff like this doesn't happen around here. Not to me."

"It is normal on Osborne. Visitors are celebrated, just like Osbornians are celebrated when we visit alternates. It is like we are—" It frowned, searched for a word—"Cousins!"

That made Sam smile. He didn't have any cousins. Not close ones, anyway. His were further down the family tree, though not as distant as Flum.

"Do you have a family back home?"

More sobbing. This time Flum hugged Sam until it could talk again. "I have a Noma and a Thrimm and Pelli. Noma is parent, Thrimm is parent, and Pelli is just Pelli."

"A sister?" Sam asked, thinking it sounded like a girl's name.

Flum shook its head.

"Brother?"

Another shake. "We do not have genders assigned as you do. Not boy, not girl. We are each once."

Sam leaned back as he tried to take this in. "All of you? Are you born…the same?"

"We are all once," Flum insisted.

Sam understood. Osbornians were one gender, but that didn't mean they were carbon copies of each other. "Here when we have boy and girl genders we say, 'him' and 'her'. What do I call you?"

Flum shrugged. "On Osborne we are genders neutral."

A lightbulb flashed. "We have gender neutral! I can call you 'them' and 'they.' Will that be okay?"

Flum nodded. "You are the first person to speak to me. I must find my shift so I can get back! My family will be so worried."

Sam had no way to guess how old Flum was, but they sounded young. "Do you go to school on Osborne?"

Flum nodded. "I am in my seventh year."

"Same as me! Just about. Are you twelve years old?"

"Thirteen." They hiccupped. "Thirteen last Monday. My Noma made a Shnummy cake."

"That sounds...good?"

They nodded again, glum.

The sun continued its trek across the sky as they shared details of their worlds. Sam thought it was incredible that they spoke the same language, but Flum explained it wasn't like that.

"Once upon a shift, great effort was made to hide and observe and study a language before a friendship was made. Now we have this." From beneath their collar, they pulled a leather string attached to a carved wooden figure that looked like a distorted letter *F*.

"What's that?"

"It is what we use when language does not match."

"You're saying that this is magic too?" Sam felt like his brain had been turned inside out. When he was little, he'd loved the idea of magic and was fascinated especially by Icelandic stories of trolls and elves and sorcerers. But he'd left those ideas behind. "Magic" was all tricks and illusion done by talented performers.

Flum rubbed their thumb against the pendant. "This

magic is a teaching from our Wise One for travellers. I hear your words in my language, and you hear my language in yours."

"Your...Wise One gave this to you?"

Their face fell again. "Not this one. I did not expect to travel and so did not bring one with me. I made it from your tree. I had to." A fat tear dribbled down their bulbous cheek. Tentatively, Sam patted their knee. Flum smiled gratefully.

Sam's brain worked furiously to grasp something familiar that would keep him from tipping over the edge of something he feared was too deep to climb out of. Magic was not real! It couldn't be. Of all the impossible things that had happened this week, this was too much.

Or was it? An idea glimmered and fought its way to the surface from a murky swamp of all that was muddled and nonsensical.

"In the old days people would have thought airplanes were magic, like, if one went back in time. I think magic is just science we still need to learn about. Like you."

Flum grinned.

His brain worked so hard he thought steam might come out of his ears. He turned Flum's pendant back and over in his hands. "This carving works like a translation app!"

Flum either knew about apps or didn't care. They probably had to accept a whole lot of new things when they visited other worlds. It was like when Sam read a book and came across a word he didn't know. He would either stop and look it up or keep reading and eventually figure out the meaning through context.

"There are many things the same between alternates, like trees and water and dogs," Flum said. "The joy is in discovering what is different." They grabbed hold of Sam's arms. "This was a new shift, and I discovered it! Flum! Mapping shifts is something Osbornians love to do. I will get to name it." Flum settled back against the bench and sighed. "If I get back. This is my first solo alternate. You're not supposed to find a new one as your first solo. In case of complications."

"Complications?"

"This is a complication. I've lost the shift."

Sam jumped as a voice called out, "Hello, Sam!"

He'd had been so engrossed he hadn't noticed the approaching parents and kids. Sam recognized the one who'd greeted him as the new kindergarten teacher, Ms. Johnson. She and her daughter had moved into a house three streets over at the start of the summer. It had been old Mr. Byron's house for as long as Sam could remember. Mr. Byron had moved to a valley in British Columbia to be closer to his daughter, and to orchards of peaches, which were his favourite fruit.

"We are all so glad you're okay!" she said. The other two parents nodded. A small girl peeked out from behind the man's legs, while the other three kids played somersault tag beside the path.

"Thank you," Sam said. "So am I!"

"Me too!" Flum said, beaming.

The parents kept their focus on Sam. "You tell your father if there is anything we can do—"

Flum jumped up and down. "Well, as a matter of fact—"

"—we are here for you," the woman finished, still looking at Sam. The others nodded vigorously.

"Thank you."

Sam watched Flum point their finger and move toward the man. They jabbed once, and again. The man slapped at his thigh where Flum had poked, dug in his bag and brought out bug spritzer. He sprayed the air around his thigh, which made Flum fall back, coughing and sputtering.

As they strolled away, the children laughed and bounced, and Flum looked crestfallen. "You see? They pretend I'm not even here." They sniffled deeply.

"I'm pretty sure that isn't it," Sam said. "It's like they didn't see or hear you. But the dad definitely felt you poke at him."

"Dude!" a familiar voice called.

"Hi, Randy. How's the car?"

Randy chuckled as he drew close. "Made it all the way around the block this time! Really glad you're okay, little dude."

"Yeah, me too."

"You put Gilla Farm on the map! Well, sort of. You were all over the national news, but they said you were from"—he made air quotes—"just outside Winnipeg."

"Randy, I need to ask you something."

"Shoot!"

"Have you seen Thyla?"

Flum looked at him curiously. So did Randy.

"Who?"

Sam was suddenly very aware that his question made no sense to Randy.

"I...hehe...I'm just working out a joke thing. Like a play. That's why I'm wearing a costume."

Randy face cubes unscrunched. "You're in the play? I heard the suit was like protective armour or something."

The play? He'd forgotten—a group of kids from the theater club were putting on a big end-of-summer play. "Something like that."

"Hey, whatever works, man!"

He glanced down at his new friend and decided to press his luck. "Randy, do you see someone sitting next to me?" He motioned beside him, then held his hand above Flum's head. "About yay high, and blue?"

"Hallo, hallo!" Flum said, waving.

Randy tilted his head, then leaned in and peered into Sam's eyes. "They put you on something, little dude? Some kind of medicine? There's just you and me."

Sam forced a chuckle. "Just practising for the play."

Randy put his hand on Sam's shoulder. "Well, gotta get to work. You take care, okay?"

"I will."

Before Randy stood straight, Flum tickled him under his chin. Randy scratched where Flum had touched but otherwise gave no sign of noticing anything or anyone out of the ordinary.

Flum looked brighter as Randy left them. "Humans are not rude! They just don't see me."

"Except me. But you do have a solid presence for touching things."

Flum looked perplexed. "Strange." They took a small notebook and pencil from their satchel, wrote something, and tucked it back inside.

"Beyond strange," Sam agreed. "There's also the thing about Thyla."

Flum cocked their head to one side.

"Thyla is my neighbour, but for everyone except me it's like she never existed, except she did. Does. Like you!"

"Magic?" Flum asked.

"Or science that no one has figured out yet." Sam thought back to everything Flum had told him. "You've been here for three nightfalls. Since Monday?"

Flum nodded.

"When you came through the shift, did you see lots of people and flashing lights?"

Flum nodded again.

"That was when I was hit by lightning. The lightning changed something in my brain. Maybe that's why I can see and hear you, and other people can't."

Flum lifted their brows high. "Electromagnetic discharges can stimulate a shift. Your brain, and my shift! I already know so much more than I did. I believe you will help me find my way home."

"Could it also mean that I only imagined Thyla?"

Flum's bushy brows came together as they thought. "You are not forgetting, you are remembering. Your brain is seeing more, not less."

It made so much sense he wanted to cry. "My seeing you is thanks to electromagnetic stuff, and not my brain gone bonkers. It's science!" Sam felt like doing handstands.

As they left Omega Park and walked down Main Street, Flum was like an odd-shaped bloodhound, sniffing everything, and howling with delight. No one noticed. "Earth smells so interesting! Different than Osborne, and different from every other alternate."

Manju and her dog caught up with them. "Hey, Sam,

how're you doing?" she asked, while her dog sniffed at Flum and wagged her tail. This delighted Flum, who held out their palm for a sniff.

"I'm good!" said Sam, waiting for Manju to notice Finny's sniffing, and maybe Flum.

"That was so crazy what happened. Glad you're okay." She touched his sleeve and smiled. "This is fancy."

"Thanks, it's a conductive suit." He decided to make a joke out of it. "You know, just in case I'm suddenly some super lightning attractor. Just trying it out."

Manju smiled again. "Sounds like a good idea." She whistled to Finny. "Gotta go!"

"Wait!"

Manju turned.

"Do you remember a girl named Thyla from our school?"

She shook her head.

"Okay, thanks."

Manju and her dog trotted off.

"Four people and one dog. No one remembers Thyla, and only the dog saw you."

"With its nose!"

"It must all be connected."

Flum shrugged again.

"The scientist must ask a testable question."

Flum looked utterly confused.

"It's a nine-point scientific method. I did it backwards, but I think my question should be: What do my eyes, you, and Thyla's disappearance have in common."

"What is the answer?"

"That's only step one. Step two is to use reliable information, and step three is to make a hypothesis."

Flum's eyes waggled back and forth, and Sam imagined them searching for right translation. "A guess?"

"An *educated* guess."

"Do you have one?"

Sam nodded, so excited he could feel his shoulders and fingertips buzzing. "Three things that have never happened before began with the lightning strike. The hypothesis is this: My wonky eyes, your appearance, and Thyla's disappearance were all caused by the lightning."

"What do we do next?"

"We are supposed to make a plan."

"A plan to get me home!"

Sam's shoulders fell. He hadn't a clue how to make that happen, but he would keep his wonky eyes and electromagnetic infused brain open. Maybe he'd inherited some figuring-things-out genes from his dad.

They passed four more people on the sidewalk and three cars with occupants who waved and called hello. Everyone was friendly and concerned. No one noticed Flum. At the abandoned playhouse, they spotted the theatre students who would stage the end-of-summer play. It was going to be about the history of Gilla Farm.

"Sam!" a teenager called.

He looked familiar. "Dennis McKerlie?" Sam asked. Dennis graduated high school two years ago and won a TV stand-up comedy competition. He'd moved to Toronto but came back sometimes to visit his parents. He looked way different from when he'd gone to their school.

"Yeah," he threw his head back and laughed. "I guess you're a celebrity after what happened. Everyone knows you, but you don't know everyone."

"I know who you are. Everyone does! Did you shave your head?"

Dennis grinned and rubbed a hand over where he used to have long black curls.

Out the corner of his eye, Sam saw Flum do the same to their own hairless blue head.

"For a role," Dennis said. "I was in a commercial!"

"That's an awesome suit," a girl said. Paula Maclean was tall and red haired. Like Thyla, she'd graduated last year. "You could be one of our actors. Spaceman Sam!"

"It's a conductive suit," he mumbled.

"Hey, that's a great idea!" Dennis said. "Sam, you are now a part of the history of Gilla Farm. Want to be in the show?"

"I don't know. What if I had a"—he glanced at Flum—"a sidekick? Someone from another world."

Dennis and Paula tilted their heads in unison. "It's a true story, Sam," Paula said.

"What if I said this was true?"

Dennis laughed and patted Sam's shoulder. "Funny guy! Think about joining us, okay? This is a community project. The more the merrier."

Dennis and Paula joined the other students inside the theatre, leaving Sam and Flum alone on the step. Flum scratched another note in their notebook.

Sam was the only one who could see Flum, which meant he was the only chance his new friend had to get back home.

CHAPTER TEN

PIXEL PERFECT

Sam put his fingers to his lips, glanced around to make sure no one was watching, and opened the back door.

"I thought no ones could see me," Flum said.

"But they can see me," Sam whispered.

Flum giggled. "They see you sneaking into your house?"

Sam frowned, cleared his throat, and stood straight. This hanging out with an invisible creature from another world would take some getting used to. "Dad, you home?" he called.

"In the kitchen!" came the reply. "How was your walk?"

"Interesting," he said with a glance at Flum, then, "Good!"

"Good! Hungry?"

"Um...sure! How long until dinner?"

"Twenty minutes!"

Sam smiled apologetically at Flum, who had their hands over their ears. "Sorry," he whispered. "Don't people shout on Osborne?"

Flum let go of their ears and shook their head. "If we need to talk to someone who is not near, we magic there."

Sam sighed. "We don't have magic on Earth, Flum. Not the kind you mean. That sounds like a teleporter. We haven't figured out how to do that yet."

He pulled open the basement door and motioned for Flum to follow. He flipped on the light, closed the door behind them and said nothing more until they were at the bottom of the stairs. "I can make you a hiding place here," he said.

"But if no ones can see me, why do I hide?"

"If Dad sees me talking to you, he'll think I'm talking to myself and will take me back to the hospital for more tests. If we're going to figure out how to get you back home, I can't keep going back and forth to the hospital."

Flum nodded, but they didn't look happy as they peered into the shadows of the basement. From a floor-to-ceiling set of wooden shelves, Sam pulled out a cardboard box. "I've got a blanket in here." He pulled out his baby blanket and held it up to Flum. "Too small for me now, but it should keep you warm."

Flum took the blanket from Sam. They turned it this way and that, and ran their blue fingers along the pattern, "I know this," they said.

"It was my mother's favourite pattern. It's Icelandic. Do you have something like it on Osborne?"

"Exactly like it," they said. "It is for protection."

"Yes!" Sam said. Remembering how Flum had called Thursday "Thor's Day," he dug back in the box and pulled out a book of myths. "My dad thinks this stuff is silly, but I used to like it. Can you read it with your, um, translation thingy?"

Flum pulled the pendant from beneath their collar. "It is called *Ansuz*," they said. "It is rune magic."

Sam frowned. *Rune magic*?

While Flum flipped through the book of myths, Sam dug back in the box and pulled out another book. It was called *Runology* and explained how the old Norse god Odin had got hold of these symbols, called runes. It also told how in ancient times Vikings had used them to leave messages all over Europe. He flipped to the back of the book and found the page he was looking for. There it was: Ansuz. Beside the word there was a picture of the very pendant Flum had carved, and the words, "god's mouth," and "communication."

"I always thought runes were like an old alphabet," Sam said. There was no mention of magic in the books, except for the part about the Norse gods. The book treated those stories more like history than something made up. There were some adults who believed in magic, and they wrote books like this. There were no Templetons amongst them, of this Sam was sure.

"They are that and it is more, but I am still learning," Flum said.

"It's like you said, I guess. There are lots of things the same between alternates." Except that Flum believed in magic, and people on Earth, once they were old enough to know better, did not.

He wondered if Dory had known about rune magic and its use in Icelandic myths. Not for the first time, he wished he knew more about her. The real her, not what was packed up and left behind in boxes.

Flum poked through the jumble of books and action

figures and settled with delight on a blue rubber troll with yellow floss hair. Sam had forgotten it was there. Flum peered more closely, then pulled at its stubby arms.

"It's like someone tried to make a toy that looked like you, but missed," Sam offered.

Sadness was something Sam didn't need eyes to see. It rolled off his strange new companion in waves as they stared at the toy troll.

"Are you thinking about your family?"

They nodded and sighed loudly. "What if I can't get back?" Their eyes filled with tears.

Sam didn't know what to say. He picked up the doll. "Your arms are longer." He touched his finger in the same spot Flum had and experienced a soft jolt. "Oh!" he cried. It was the same sensation as when he held a finger on a phone app icon to shift it into edit mode. He half expected a small "x" to appear beside the spot. Still touching, he wiggled his fingertip and was startled to notice a space appear between the pixels. "Oh!" he said again and jerked his hand away. A shimmer appeared between the pixels and slowly filled in.

Whoa!

Flum snatched the doll back and pulled at the adjusted arm. "You made it longer!" They handed it back. "Do the other one!"

Sam tapped at the other arm. "Nothing," he said. No jolt. No space created no matter how much he wiggled his fingertip. "Wait. You touched this arm before I did. Try that."

Flum tapped the other arm. Sam did the same. There it was—the jolt. "Whatever this is, it needs both of us to work!"

Sam wiggled his fingertip until another space appeared. He pulled his touch away and saw the space fill with a shimmering new pixel.

It must have something to do with remnants of electricity left in his body. Flum must have picked up the same electricity when they arrived.

But what they could do with it was too much for his mind to bend around. There would be time to think more deeply later. For now he would go with it.

He touched the arm again, then again, widening each new pixel before it turned solid. Soon his troll doll had two arms that hung down to its knees. He adjusted again here and there, until it was a pretty good likeness to Flum, at least in shape. The doll had hair but no eyebrows, while Flum had brows and no hair.

"My Noma." Flum held the doll close, eyes glistening.

Sam felt a pull in his heart. "You keep the doll until you get home."

"Will I get home?" A tear spilled over.

"We'll find a way. Maybe this touch-thing will help."

Something sparked in Flum. "Together we will find the shift!"

"This is all so weird," Sam said. "Before I met you, I wouldn't have believed you were possible."

"I am possible."

"Some people would say that I've lost my marbles."

"We will find them!"

"No," Sam put out a hand to stop Flum from searching. "It's just a saying. But my friend Derek would say that in the great cosmic plan of the universe, this is meant to be." Flum, his new world-shifting friend, needed to get home.

And maybe, just maybe, Sam was their answer. "We'll figure it out, Flum. I promise."

Eyes alight, Flum held up a thumb. Solemnly, Sam shook it. He felt another soft jolt.

"Together," they said in unison.

"Sam? Are you down here?"

Sam looked up to see his father peering down the stairs. "Yup! Right here!" He quickly clasped the troll doll so it wouldn't look like it was floating in mid-air while held by Flum. "Just going through some of my old stuff."

"Do you want a hand?" Dad asked and started down the stairs.

"Nope, nu-uh. All good!" Sam said. "Be right up."

There was a creak as Dad stopped and shifted his weight. "Okay. Come wash for dinner."

"You bet! I'll, uh, just put this away first."

Dad nodded and disappeared back upstairs. Sam listened, but there was no sound of a closing door. He must have left it open.

"Why would he give you his hand?" Flum asked. "Won't he need it?"

Sam grinned. "Just another expression," he whispered, hoping he was quiet enough that Dad wouldn't hear through the open door. "It means that he wanted to help." He picked up the blanket and handed it again to Flum. "I'll get you a pillow later."

Flum threw their arms around Sam and pleaded. "No, please no!" they cried. "I do not like this place! Please do not leave me all on my own."

Sam peered into the shadows, noticing the cobwebs and dust. He wouldn't like to sleep here either.

"Okay, you can stay in my room. But you have to be quiet. I will sneak you something to eat after I clean up the supper dishes."

Sam put the box away, minus the blanket, the *Runology* book, and the troll. Flum pressed the doll tightly to their chest before tucking it in their satchel.

"Thank you, Sam. Thank you for your hand and your lost marbles."

CHAPTER ELEVEN

A TOUCH OF MAGIC

The next morning, Sam woke to Flum jumping up and down on their makeshift pillow-bed, eager to begin their search.

Sam rubbed his eyes and yawned. "Remember to be careful about moving stuff when Dad is around."

Quivering, Flum held out Sam's book of Sagas. It was open to the first page. "Saemundur!" they squealed.

Sam cringed again until he remembered that only he could hear Flum. He rubbed his eyes again and saw Flum tapping on the pencilled-in word. "Do you know what it is?" Maybe Flum's translation thingy had uncovered its secret.

"It is our Wise One," they said. "Wise One is a Sister of Saemunder."

"You know this Saemunder?"

Flum shook their head.

"Then how do you know your Wise One is his or her or their sister?"

Flum grinned. "The Sisters of Saemunder are," they furrowed their brow, "a group."

Sam glanced at the word, and back at Flum, who stared expectantly back at him. "Interesting. What does it mean that someone wrote the group's name in this book?"

Flum shrugged then jumped up and down again. "Something!"

"Maybe it's like dogs and trees, the same on your world as mine. But I've never heard of a Sister of Saemunder group."

"She is a protector of magic."

"*She*? She is not gender-one?"

"She is not from Osborne. She came to Osborne to teach."

"From where?"

"She does not say."

"Huh." He looked again at the word and wondered who wrote it. Had a Sister of Saemunder visited Earth too? "We have enough mystery on our plate for now."

Flum grinned and rubbed their belly. "A plate! Yes please."

Sam peeked out his bedroom window and saw Dad disappear into his shed. "Coast is clear."

After a quick breakfast of oatmeal with banana, Sam pulled on his conductive suit and they were out the door.

Dad was trimming the front shrubs. "Samuel! You seem well today. How's your vision?"

He wanted to tell Dad about his new ability to move pixels, but he could hardly do that without talking about Flum. Flum, who only Sam could see. If he tried to explain, Dad would pack him in the car and whisk him right back to the hospital and lock him away until he was normal again. Okay, maybe not that, but for sure he'd want to run more tests. "Same vision," he said instead. "But it's okay. I'm used to it."

Dad frowned. "I am glad you've adjusted." Except he didn't look glad.

"Is that wrong?"

Flum tugged at him, urging him away.

"No, not at all! It's just that adjustment isn't what we're going for. Come up to my office and I'll examine you." He brightened. "I've been going over my old research and began cross-referencing—"

Flum tugged harder. "Dad," Sam interrupted, "we're just going to the park."

Eyebrow vees again.

"I mean, I'm going. Guess the pixels are getting me mixed up, hehe."

His father's shoulders slumped. "Oh, yes. It's good that you're getting out."

"But as soon as I get back, okay?"

Smile cubes. "Okay."

He and Flum dashed away before Sam got himself in any additional word trouble.

As they passed the old theatre, Dennis called out. He was struggling with a wide-bodied canoe. "Hey, Spaceman Sam! Decide to join the show?"

"No. I mean, I don't know. Still thinking."

"While you're thinking, can you take the other end?" Dennis nodded toward the canoe.

"Okay."

"Thanks! We're always light on extra hands before lunch."

Sam locked his fingers under the keel and lifted. It wasn't heavy, but its length proved awkward. Once they got it through the front door, there was a step and a turn to maneuver around. "Hang on, Sam, I just—"

Sam waited.

"Okay, now—"

Sam moved.

From inside: "Yow!"

Sam stopped. "You okay?"

"Yep." But Dennis's voice sounded choked. "Back it up."

Sam moved backward.

"Now forward."

Sam moved forward.

"Okay, okay, okay," Dennis said as they inched through.

"Stop!" Sam called, seeing he was about to lose his knuckles against the doorframe.

A muffled laugh from inside. "I'm not good at measurements. I guess we should have had someone who understands physics check out the angle first."

Physics, or maybe pixels, Sam thought. "Wait a second, Dennis! I have an idea."

"If you could see me now." Another laugh. "Trust me, I'm not going anywhere. Backward or forward."

Sam looked around for Flum. They were near the snack table holding a glass of lemonade and sniffing a jar of peanut butter. "*Psst,*" Sam called, trying not to think of how weird and scary it would be for anyone watching to see a floating glass.

"You say something?" Dennis asked.

"Nope!" He placed the weight of the canoe on his knee, then took his freed hand and waved wildly at Flum.

Mrs. Ruth-Ann Sabourin was passing by with her two small dogs, Teddy and Kimmie. "Hello, Sam," she called, and waved back.

"H-hello, Mrs. Ruth-Ann." She insisted everyone use

her first name, no matter their age. Sam always felt funny about that, so stuck a "Mrs." in front.

"Good to see you out and about."

"Sure."

"Is that heavy?"

"Nope. Not too bad."

Flum joined him, noisily smacking their fingers. Sam smelled peanut butter.

"Like Shnummy, but different!" they said. Teddy and Kimmie sniffed the air. To Sam, the dogs looked like fuzzy grey and white slippers on invisible feet. They even moved that way, one moving a little ahead then falling back as the other moved ahead. Right now, the invisible feet were still.

Mrs. Ruth-Ann stood there awkwardly, as if waiting for Sam to say something else, until Kimmie started jumping up against her knee in an un-slipper like way. "We'd better move along. Goodbye!"

"Bye." He must remember that no one else could see Flum, and that meant no more wild waving!

As she walked away, Sam pointed to where his knuckles were about to disappear in the doorframe. "Touch here," he whispered.

Flum did. With his free hand Sam touched the same spot. There was a soft jolt, and a space appeared. Before it filled in, he waggled his fingers back and forth, making it wider. Catching on, Flum touched again, and they repeated the process until Sam could easily slide his knuckles, and the canoe, through the opening.

"Right on!" Dennis said. "For a minute I thought we'd have to rearrange the whole play around the canoe stuck halfway through the door."

"I'm sure your writers would have figured out something."

"Ha! Right on. You going to stick around?"

"We're…er, I'm going to the park."

"Interesting fact! Did you know it used to be called Odal Park? Odal was the name of a medieval rune, but after the Nazis put feet on it and made it one of their symbols of hate, the town council decided to change it. The Omega symbol was pretty close, so presto-change, Omega Park."

Sam's ears pricked. "Odal. You mean like the Icelandic rune?" he asked.

Denis shrugged. "Dunno. Older than Iceland, I think. Aren't runes about magic?"

"I guess," Sam said. "But in Viking times they were used as letters. Odal was for the letter 'O'." He knew that from the *Runology* book.

"Interesting. Maybe we can work that into the play. Icelandic immigrants were the first Gilla Farm townspeople, you know. Help yourself to the snack table before you go and come back any time!"

"Thanks, we will!" Oops! He'd done it again. "I mean, I will."

As they left the theatre, he and Flum swooped their fingers along the edge of the doorframe they'd altered, which now sported a dip. There was an electrical *snap!* and the frame righted itself.

As Flum hurried back to the snack table, Sam felt a sensation run through him, but not like a lightning bolt or shock of panic. He felt *useful.* He felt *special.* For at least as long as this touch thing he and Flum had lasted, they might be able to do some interesting things. What else might they discover?

On their way to Odal-Turned-Omega Park, Sam and Flum experimented with moving around pixels, but only on things—no plants or anything else alive.

They flopped onto the grass next to where the lamppost used to be.

"It's a neat trick," Sam said, "but how do we use it to find your shift?" Seeing Flum's face fall, he quickly added, "We *will* find it!"

"I already looked."

"I know, but—" Sam fanned his fingers in front of him, then touched Flum's hand. The soft jolt was becoming familiar. "Maybe it will be different if we look together. Maybe something new will happen, like with the doorframe and the doll. Maybe working together is the key."

"There is no key."

Sam put his hand on Flum's shoulder. "Another expression. Chin up. We'll figure it out."

Flum smiled, nodded, then looked to the sky, which made Sam smile too. Chin up. They were so literal.

Sam followed Flum's gaze and imagined his sight like it used to be when he would spot shapes in clouds. Now everything looked like a sliding tile game. Move this tile here and that one there, and he'd win the prize!

He returned his attention to the grass.

Within the pattern, fresh green shoots had begun to appear. This worried Sam. Eventually, everything would be back to normal—the grass, and Sam's eyes. Would he be able to see Flum when his regular eyesight returned? No one else could.

He decided not to share this new concern with Flum. They were already worried enough. If they were going to find the shift, it had better be soon.

"Every shift is different," Flum said. "Because this one is new, I don't know what to look for."

"Tell me about the others."

Sam guessed it was a favourite subject for Flum. He was right. They began to vibrate, and their eyes grew bright. "There are many. Noma once took me through the Spinolian Shift to Baffinalt, a place with shiny streets and very cold." They waggled their fingers. "It was stinging, and we wore socks on our hands." They frowned and rubbed their decoder. "Mittens."

"Ice? Were the streets ice?"

"Yes! Everything was ice. Like in a refrigerator without the box, and peoples lived there."

"We have that too, Flum. It's called winter."

Flum's eyebrows shot up. "Oh, that is wondrous! But where is it?"

"It's called a season. We have four of them, and they happen at different times. Winter, spring, summer, and fall." Sam watched as Flum thought through the translations.

"On Baffinalt it is winter all year round."

"What is it like on Osborne?"

"It would be your summer. Like now. Except for us it is always. Another difference." They retrieved their notebook and wrote another line.

Sam wanted to know more about the worlds the shifts led to, but remembered the growing grass and disappearing pattern. "We should probably focus on the shift, Flum. How does it work?"

"Work?"

"Are shifts like doorways that you step through, like in my house? Or are they shimmery things like in movies?"

Flum looked confused. He tried again. "Shimmer, like a river going over stones. Wind on a puddle. A jiggly mirror?"

Flum smiled. "They are not the same in shape or size. They are something you catch out of the corner of your eye."

"That sounds hard to see."

"It is something you learn. Look that way," they said, pointing at the trees. "And don't turn!"

Facing the trees, he had a sense of Flum nodding even though he didn't actually see. With his head still, he shifted his eyes so that he could better see what Flum was doing.

"No! Not like that. Keep your eyes with the trees."

Sam did as he was told.

"What am I doing?" Flum asked.

"I don't know. You said I can't look."

"You don't need to. Let go of looking. What am I doing?"

Not entirely sure what Flum meant, he relaxed his eyes and stopped trying to see the tree pixels. He sunk into daydreaming. After a minute, he felt something. A feeling that was kind of like seeing. "You're rocking. Sideways back and forth, like a clock pendulum."

"Yes! Now you see."

Sam smiled, turned back to Flum. "Okay, I get it. We will find it by not looking." He sighed. "Sounds hard."

"It isn't really. Once you know the look-feel, you can't miss it." Flum's eyes again filled with tears. "Unless it is gone."

"It's okay, Flum. It'll be different with two of us looking." He waved his hand. "Maybe it blew apart in the lighting strike."

"Oh!" Now Flum looked even more worried.

"If it did blow apart, there will be pieces, right? And if there are pieces, we can fix it with our touch, just like we changed the doll, and fixed the doorframe at the theatre. Come on!"

Sam and Flum each chose a different direction and walked back and forth along an imagined grid. As they met in the middle, Sam asked, "Anything?"

Flum slumped their shoulders.

"Don't give up, Flum! Maybe like the touch thing, we have to look together."

"How? We have different eyes."

"Unless we look through a camera." He pulled out his cell phone, clicked on the camera app. Just like everything else he looked at on screen, the pixels were gone. Except it was different from a regular screen. With his camera, he could zoom.

"I don't understand how this will help," said Flum.

"It's worth a try. Come close." He pointed the camera along one branch of the fading scorch pattern. "Does this look the same through the camera as it does in real life?"

"Can't tell."

Sam zoomed into a smaller patch. "How about now?"

Flum looked through the phone lens, then outside of it, back and forth, back and forth. "Same."

"Different for me, but not in any way that can help. Let's keep trying."

They inched along a branch, reached a fork, took another branch.

"Here!" Flum cried. "It is here!" They dashed in front of the camera. "Oh, no! Not here."

"Things always look different through the camera."

Flum returned and tapped a spot on the phone screen. Sam let his eyes lose focus and saw it too. It *was* a shimmer, like a ripple in a river that changed in the light, about the size of a carrot. It was there, and not. They moved the camera closer and closer, looking but not looking, until Flum was able to reach it with their hand.

"Oh!" they cried as it moved from their touch, as if they had some sort of negative magnetic charge.

"Wait," Sam said. He held up his hand. "Together."

They touched palms until Sam felt a jolt. It was gentle and more like a pulse, as if his heart and Flum's beat together. Flum appeared to grow fuller, stronger, and there was a glow coming from them. In looking-not-looking Sam sensed that together they were a ball of light. Together, thumbs entwined, they reached for the shimmer, and grasped hold.

"Got it!" Flum cried. Sam let go and breathed a sigh of relief when the shimmer remained. Both through the camera, and outside of it, he could now see it with perfect clarity.

It was a long diamond shape made of glass, with an ember of colour embedded deep within. Green. Maybe.

"Together," Sam said again.

He saw a brightening in Flum, and not just their eyes. "Yes," Flum said. "Yes, my friend. My friend, Sam. My true friend, Sam. Flum and Spaceman Sam." Flum tucked the shard in their satchel.

"It worked, Flum. Together, we will find your way home."

Then his phone died.

CHAPTER TWELVE

FAMILY TRADITION

Dad shone a penlight in Sam's eyes and made him turn his head one way, then the other. He wrote notes on a clipboard. "No change in the pixelated vision?"

There was a big change from the last time Dad checked his eyes, but not the way he meant. His other-world friend sat in Dad's office chair and swung their legs.

"Nope. Everything's the same."

"Okay. That's good for today. I need to pop by the Institute." His pixels were vibrating again. "Get your shoes on. It shouldn't take long."

"Can I stay here?"

Dad paused before answering while Sam tried not to be distracted by Flum, who hopped off the chair, stood on their tiptoes and peeked at Dad's clipboard before wandering out of sight down the hall.

"I don't see why not. Just make sure—"

Whatever Dad was going to tell him was interrupted by a crash from the kitchen. *Flum!* Dad frowned and followed the noise, Sam at his heels.

"Oh no!" Sam cried. Dory's favourite platter was in

shards on the kitchen floor. Flum had flattened themselves against the wall, looking both guilty and contrite.

"Strange," Dad said. "I'm sure I left this well back from the counter edge."

"Maybe an earthquake. Sometimes earthquakes have tremors that travel incredible distances, isn't that right, Dad?" He was speaking too fast and forced himself to slow down. "Could happen. Right?" He chided himself for not saying *train*. That would have been more believable.

There was a softening of the confusion on Dad's face. "Sam, if there is something you want to tell me, you should. I won't get mad. Accidents happen."

He thought it was Sam's fault. If he tried to deny it, he would only make things worse. Dad knew something was up. Better to let him think it was this.

"But it was Dory's favourite," he said.

Dad pulled the broom and dustpan out of the closet.

"Let me do that." Sam reached for the broom. "I'm sorry. I was looking at it and must have left it too close to the edge. I didn't mean for it to fall."

"There is construction going on next door. If the tray was close too the edge, vibrations from equipment might have rattled it over."

"Construction?"

"The Smiths are renovating. I believe they are turning their spare bedroom into an office, or maybe a sauna. I heard Mrs. Cooper talking about it when I was in buying bread. She didn't know the details. If the Smiths feel it's anyone's business, I expect we'll hear soon enough." Dad frowned. "I wouldn't think they'd use a jackhammer or any large equipment that might cause a vibration." He shrugged. "But what do I know about construction?"

Thyla's room! Sam thought with alarm. It had to be. Just one step deeper into the mystery of why no one remembered her, not even her mom and dad. It was as if the universe was tying up loose ends.

Dad bent and picked up a perfectly round piece. It was the pattern!

And it glowed.

So that was weird.

"Do you see that?" Sam asked.

"The pattern? Sure I do."

"The light."

Dad followed Sam's line of sight. "There's no light, Samuel. Just the etching. Oh!" He uttered a soft cry as the piece broke in his hand.

Sam watched the glow begin to dull and melt from the clay into his father's hand. He glanced at Flum, whose eyes were wide. Sam wasn't the only one who'd seen it.

"I guess it cracked during the fall. I'm sorry, Son."

"Why?"

"You don't have many mementos of your mother. I wish now we hadn't sold that piano bench. I guess we don't think of some things until they are gone."

Except Thyla. Not too many people thinking of her.

Sam shrugged. "Things are just things. The stuff that really matters is what's inside of us."

A memory twigged. *Everything you need is inside of you.* It was the phrase that had come to him in the park.

His father had a strange expression on his face. "Dad? Is something wrong?"

"No, it's just that you remind me so much of your mother."

"We have the same eyebrows."

"It's more than that." Dad sat in his chair. "It's the way you say things. And what you say."

"What do I say?"

He paused again. "Beyond that very wise comment you just made about what's important, it's your enthusiasm. Even when things are tough, you want to get right out there, jump into the middle of things. Like wanting to help with chores despite your vision. And how you were afraid to go outside, but instead of giving in to that, you thought up your suit. It's a good quality, Samuel. I love it in you, and I loved it in your mother."

Sam thought about this. No one had ever told him what he was like. As far as he was concerned, he was just Sam. But now he knew he was like his mother. It made him feel closer to her. He didn't know if that made him feel better, or worse that he didn't remember her.

"Why did she leave, Dad? I mean, why then? Did something happen?"

"Her uncle died."

Sam knew his mother's uncle had raised her after her parents died when she was still very young. He also knew she had no brothers or sisters. "But why didn't she come back?"

His father shook his head. He looked up and pulled a thick book from the shelf above his desk. Inside the front flap was a thin envelope with a single sheet of pink paper. "I've read this over and over, thinking there must be some sort of clue." He handed it to Sam. "There isn't."

It was his mother's letter. He'd seen it many times and knew by heart what it said.

> *I can't explain. Please tell our boy that I love him, that I will always love him. I love you too. Please don't try to find me. I won't write again.*

That was all, except for an "xo" at the end. He handed it back.

"Tell me again how you tried to find her."

"I phoned the police, hotels in Reykjavik—"

"The capital—"

"And only city—"

"And in her uncle's village," Sam added.

"I wrote letters to her extended family—"

"And the town hall, and the library." Sam knew this story inside out.

"No one could help, and because of her letter, the police decided she left of her own accord, which meant she wasn't missing."

"Except to us."

They were both quiet. Sam wished there was something else, some forgotten clue, but there was nothing.

"Grandpa and Grandma in Toronto told me stories of your cousins and uncles. But it's like her side of the family isn't even real."

"It only seems like that because you never met them." He returned to the shelf and pulled down a tin box. He flipped the lid and pulled out a postcard. "From her great-aunt, Halla Haraldsdottir."

> *Let her go. She is her way. Fate for you and the boy.*

Sam frowned. "What does that even mean?"

Dad smiled. "She was getting on in age and didn't use English very often in her village. I believe she meant that your mother needed to follow her own path, and that her path is different from ours. Old Halla was a kind woman, but she refused to tell me anything more."

"How is that kind?"

Dad pulled out more postcards. There were eight. Four with the words, *Gleðileg jól,* and four with the words, *Hamingju með afmælið til drengsins.*

He separated the cards into two groups of four. "I put the phrases through a translator website. These say 'Merry Christmas,' in Icelandic, and these say, 'Happy birthday to the boy.' She wrote every year. Only someone who wishes you well would do that. I wrote back, but she never responded. When the cards stopped coming, I called her village. She'd passed away."

Sam thought sadly of the old aunt he never knew, about how she reached out to him, a boy she'd never met. "Why didn't she use my name?"

"I don't know. Just how she spoke, I guess."

Sam flipped the cards over to look at the pictures of volcanoes and sheep. Each had what looked like a hand-drawn pattern in a corner: The Helm of Awe. "The same one Dory liked."

"I wonder if it's a family thing. Like a coat of arms, or a tartan." Dad handed him the box. "You can hang onto these, if you like. I always intended that you'd have them one day."

Sam took the box and tucked the cards back inside. "Is there anyone else in her family?"

"No one close. Your mother only kept in touch with her uncle and her great-aunt. You can read about the others here." Dad reached to his computer, tapped on the keyboard and pulled up a database. "This is her Icelandic family tree. It has links to information pages about everyone in it. Icelanders are known for keeping very good family records. See? You're in here too."

Reading his name on the record connected to his mother and all these other people made him feel better somehow.

"If you click on 'ancestors' you can choose any of these names and get more information. Sometimes there are stories posted about them, like what they did for a living, and any unusual events."

Sam felt his eyes grow wide. These were his mother's ancestors, and therefore his too, even if the names didn't match. He already knew that they had a different way of using last names in Iceland. Last names began with the first name of the father and ended with "son" if they were boys, or "dottir" if they were girls. There were many, many people with the last name "Jonsdottir" and they were not all related. Not closely, anyway.

"If we were in Iceland, I would be Sam Gordonson." No one would even know that he was also the son of Dory.

"Why don't you explore that site while I'm gone? We can talk more when I get back."

Sam felt a glow inside. "That would be great!"

No sooner had Sam heard the front door shut behind his father than he heard the refrigerator door. Flum appeared with a jar of peanut butter and a handful of celery stalks, which they dipped and crunched while Sam clicked through names. "You will remember that you can't carry stuff when Dad's around, right?"

"I will." Flum pushed an extra chair to the desk and

joined Sam in examining the information on Dad's computer screen. When they glopped peanut butter next to the keyboard, they scooped it on their thumb and stuck it in their mouth, then pushed the offending jar away to avoid an unpleasant keyboard complication.

"You can read this?" Sam asked.

Flum nodded and tapped their medallion.

Only some of the descriptions were written in English. For the Icelandic parts, he pulled up a translation website and fed in sentences to convert to English. He learned that one of his great-great-great-grandfathers was a poet, and that a great-aunt wrote an important book. He read and read but did not see anything that could tell him who his mother really was. What did she like? Did anything scare her?

He dug back further. As he scanned names and listings, he found himself drawn to one over all others. He clicked on the name "Gottskalk Nikulasson" and saw a photo of an ancient-looking book beside the name. He scanned the page and felt his blood run cold. He read out loud, "Gottskalk the Cruel was the evilest man who ever lived."

Sam looked at Flum, wide eyed. "It says he wrote a book about dark magic."

Flum looked confused.

"What's wrong?" Sam asked.

"I don't know what that means. Magic is wisdom."

In Sam's mind he added "Magic isn't real" but he kept it to himself. Osbornians believed it, and it wasn't up to Sam to try and wreck what someone else believed.

Flum looked again at what was written, then back at Sam. "But this says the magic from an evil man is dark.

Dark is a shade of light. I don't understand. Why on Earth is dark bad?"

Sam shrugged. "I don't know. Language is weird."

He read on about this ancestor evil magician from the 1400s who took the form of a wolf and devoured anyone who came onto his land.

Sam turned to Flum. "It's just stories."

Flum looked grave. "And this story is in your family."

When he clicked on the icon of the book, an image of a hairy face filled the screen. It looked half human, and half wolf. The eyes bore into Sam's, and he wished for the first time that what he saw on the screen was pixelated. A shiver began at the base of his spine and moved up and through him, growing stronger in waves. He was frozen and unable to look away. A dizziness came over him as the face became fuller, rounder. It appeared to rise from the page, as if it would soon pop out of the screen.

The computer went black.

Flum was next to the desk, a power cord in their hand.

Sam exhaled and licked his lips, which had become dry. "Why did you unplug it?"

"You didn't answer. I was calling you. And then you started to make this." Flum made a choked, keening sound. "*Eeeeeee.* You got stuck in your eyes and I thought the sound meant you tried to move but you couldn't." They held up the cord and grinned. "I fixed it!"

Sam shook his head. "It must be part of the injury to my eyes," he said. "Some people have seizures when they see some kind of lights." He patted Flum's shoulder, worried about what Dad would say. "Thank you. You did fix it."

Sam wanted to read more about his ancestors, but what

if he had another seizure? Better to tell his father about it before he spent any more time online.

"I think we should do something else, Flum."

Flum bobbed their head up and down. "We will look for the shift?"

"Soon. I was thinking about Thyla."

"The girl who does not exist."

"Except she does. We've already made a hypothesis that my eyes, Thyla's disappearance, and you coming through the shift are connected, we just don't know how. The only part we haven't explored yet is the mystery of Thyla. If we find out something about her, maybe it will help us with the other two parts."

"You are very helpful."

"Not always," Sam admitted. "Not about Thyla, anyway."

"Why?"

He sighed. "I always thought Dad wished she was his kid instead of me."

"Why?"

"Because she's super smart."

"You're smart."

"Thanks, Flum, but not in the same way. The brains I do have tell me that if we are going to find out something about Thyla, we need to explore her room before the Smiths turn it into an office or whatever."

"A suna."

Sam grinned. "Sauna, Flum. I'm glad to know you were listening." He unplugged his phone from where it was charging and popped it in his jeans pocket. "Come on. We've got some spy work to do."

CHAPTER THIRTEEN

GET A CLUE

There were no clues in the Smiths' backyard. Not a blade of grass was out of place on the neatly trimmed lawn. Everything looked the same as it always did. As if nothing had happened. As if Thyla were still there.

The house was a bungalow with two windows tucked beside a back door. It was a mirror of Sam's house, which meant one window was attached to the kitchen, and the other, a bedroom. In the front there were three windows: one for the living room, another for the bathroom, and last for a bedroom. Flum hopped up on the back step and rapped loudly on the door.

"Flum!"

"Making sure no ones are home."

Sam waited until his heart stopped hammering before he responded. "Right. Good idea. Just warn me next time, okay? I need to make up a reason for being here."

"Because you are worried."

Sam softened. "Yes, I am. But what would I tell them I am worried about? Thyla doesn't exist for them, remember?"

"You should tell them."

"I wish it were that easy." He studied the back of the house and pointed. "I think that's her room." He'd often seen her sitting in the window frame with the screen popped out, feet dangling over the edge like it was a bench. She'd watch birds visiting their bird feeder, sketch, and make notes in a notebook. "Give me a boost, Flum."

Flum frowned and searched inside their sachet.

"No, I mean cup your hands like this and let me stand on them. Then you lift."

Flum grinned wide. "Yes! A boost!"

Within seconds, he was up and inside Thyla's room, standing atop her bed. That is, what should have been her bed. If the room had ever held something personal, it had been removed. He wondered if her stuff had just zapped away the moment she did.

Straining, he drew Flum up and through the window. "Maybe you should lay off the peanut butter."

Flum grinned and smacked their lips.

The room was neat, with a bare desk and floor-to-ceiling bookshelves. Unlike Sam's room, nothing was out of place.

Despite their good intentions, it felt wrong to be there. But to ask permission would only bring up questions he couldn't answer. How can you explain someone that no one remembers?

Flum tugged on his sleeve. "What are we looking for?"

"I don't know. Anything weird."

"What would be weird?"

"I don't know," he snapped. The corners of Flum's mouth pulled downward. Sam sighed. "I'm sorry. I shouldn't have said it like that. I'm just nervous."

Flum patted his hand and he felt comforted by the soft jolt.

The entire room was decorated in grey and purple. There was a soft grey carpet and a grey desk. The bed had a matching grey bedspread and purple pillows. The shelves were grey, with six drawers and two cabinet doors painted purple.

He began his search with a look under the bed. No dropped threads or bird books. He opened the closet door. There were winter coats and ski pants, but nothing he remembered Thyla wearing, not that he'd been paying that much attention. These were probably Mr. and Mrs. Smith's, put away for the summer.

"Argh!" Sam growled. "This is so frustrating! Thyla's disappearance must be connected." He put his head in his hands and thought so hard he felt like his brains might pop out his ears. "Flum, is it possible that she went through the shift at the same time as you did?"

Flum shrugged. "Every shift is different. I did not see another person."

Sam frowned. "If every shift is different, is it possible she went somewhere other than Osborne?"

Flum looked miserable. "I don't think so, but—" They wailed, "I don't know! I wish I could ask our Wise One."

Sam sat down on the bed. It must be so hard for Flum, not knowing if they would get back home. "Tell me more about your Wise One. You called her a Sister of Saemunder."

Flum blinked a few times and sniffed. "She has been there for as long as I can remember."

"And you have no idea where she came from?"

"She left her home to protect others and said that if

Osbornians would allow her to stay, she would teach us many things."

A shadow clouded Sam's mind—a fear for his friend and their family. "If she went all the way to Osborne, does that mean that she is hiding? What if someone bad is after her?"

Flum understood. "You are worried something bad might happen to Osbornians because she is there?"

"Well, yeah."

"Our elders spoke with her for many days. Osbornians discussed and voted and decided she could stay." A bright smile split their face. "Without our Wise One, we would never have known about alternates and shifts!" Their face fell. "And I would be home."

There was something else. "It's weird that someone wrote Saemunder on my book of Sagas. Is it possible your Wise One visited Earth? Maybe she taught someone here." In his mind he added, "Dory." Could Flum's Wise One have visited Earth, taught Dory about shifts, and that made her want to try one? It would explain why Dad hadn't been able to find her.

"I will ask her when I see her." Flum's eyes began to water. "If I see her."

Sam put a hand on their shoulder. "Don't worry Flum. We'll figure this out." He looked around the room. "But we won't figure it out here. We should go."

Flum nodded and followed Sam back to the window.

"You first this time." He held tight and lowered Flum through the window toward the ground.

"Want to tell me exactly what's going on here?" a voice asked.

Sam froze, then twisted his head around to see. It wasn't Mr. Smith, nor any other neighbour. This man wore the distinctive uniform of the Royal Canadian Mounted Police. Not the red dress serge they used in parades, but still recognizable: grey shirt, dark pants with a stripe. It was the stripe that gave it away. Definitely RCMP.

Sam dropped Flum, who landed with a soft "Oof."

CHAPTER FOURTEEN

STOP, DROP AND RUN!

If he'd been smart like Dad or Thyla, he would have come up with an excuse that totally made sense. But he had nothing. Instead, he panicked, rolled to the ground and yelled to Flum, "RUN!"

"What the—?" The constable stepped back in surprise. "Stop!"

Sam dashed through the back gate and down the alley. Flum was on his heels, surprisingly swift despite their short legs.

The constable was fifteen steps behind, though his wide belly slowed him through the gate. Sam saw he was puffing.

Why had they run? Everything in him shouted *Wrong! Wrong! Wrong!* But run they had, and they couldn't stop now.

"This way, Flum!" They darted into another back yard, sailed past a shed and through a front gate into the street. Two doors down they doubled back through that yard and back gate, then zigged into another yard. Puffing, they finally stopped and pressed themselves against a sunflower yellow house, hidden behind a thick stand of giant Shasta daisies. They peered into the street. "There he is," Sam whispered.

The officer looked up and down. They watched as he pulled out a handheld radio and spoke into it. *Uh oh.*

"Ha-choo!" Flum honked.

"Bless you," Sam said automatically.

The constable jerked his head toward them, and the chase was back on. This time Sam led them into the forest beyond the village toward Omega Park. The trees lining the river were thick with underbrush and a good place to hide. If that constable had called for backup, no police car could chase them through the woods. Not that Gilla Farm had a lot of backup officers at their small detachment, but there would be some.

They stopped short on reaching a padlocked gate. Fencing extended on either side like broad and impenetrable wings.

"Rats!" Sam cried.

Flum looked to and fro, clearly hoping to catch a glimpse of the beady-eyed creatures. "Where?"

"I forgot they put a service road in here." From far too close he heard shouts. The puffing RCMP officer had been joined by another. No time!

"Quick," said Sam, and touched a fence board, inviting Flum to do the same. After the zap they wiggled and pushed until they'd made a space wide enough to fit through. On the other side, they swiped and the space zapped closed.

It granted them a few extra minutes, but no more. They fought through the underbrush, then sprinted down the path. They were nearly at the playpark.

Sam had an idea—better than hiding in fireweed and willow shrubs.

The slide! Its base was shaped like the hull of a ship, fully framed with wooden boards. The inside, Sam hoped, would be hollow.

"Come on!"

They dashed across the open area to the slide. Flum guessed Sam's plan and together they made a space in the hull, hopped inside, and closed it behind them.

It was indeed hollow, but not empty. A scuffling sound in the dirt drew Sam's attention toward the back. With slivers of light bleeding through thin spaces where one board connected to the next, he saw moving darkness, and white. He turned on his phone for more light.

"Skunks!" Sam whispered.

He dared not cry out, and not because he'd heard the constables call out, "Which way?" and "He's here somewhere!" He didn't dare startle the tiny creatures. He heard a sharp inhale from Flum and saw their face split in a delighted grin. Sam squeezed their hand and shook his head. Flum frowned and turned again to the creatures. There were three very small wiggling noses. Not babies, but still young. They must have tunneled in from somewhere Sam couldn't see.

All the more reason to not move. They were lucky they hadn't been sprayed on entry.

One offered a wide yawn. What did you call a teenage skunk? A baby was called a kit. The skunklets had been sleeping, not expecting something to suddenly come through a wall. Why would they? But they were not sleeping now.

Voices right outside.

Uh-oh. How long before they figured out where they were hiding? He knew the officers could use cellphone technology to track criminals, but he wasn't that. Was he? What's a little breaking and entering between neighbours?

Technically what he did *was* a crime, but Mr. and Mrs. Smith would know that he would never steal from them.

Would they though?

What a nightmare. They couldn't pixel-nudge open the slide-boat and make a run for it. The officers might think he was some sort of demon monster coming up from the underworld and taser him! He didn't think his body could stand another electric jolt. He still ached in places he'd never thought about.

Think, think, think.

Flum tapped their fingers on the ground in a pattern the skunklets were following closely. Like kittens. Flum didn't understand this was a very bad idea.

But he'd just given Sam a very good one.

Together they could create open spaces in boards. Maybe they could also make open spaces in dirt and tunnel past their pursuers.

He held a finger to his lips then put his hand on Flum's and pushed against the earth. Flum looked confused at first, then nodded and smiled.

It worked! They made an opening in the dirt floor, small at first, then wider. More pushing, down and then under, and they had the beginnings of a tunnel. They lowered themselves inside.

"We'd better block this off before we go farther. Don't want our little friends following us."

Flum grinned.

They would close the opening and then continue to move the earth until they were out and away from the park.

The skunklings drew close and watched their progress. Just before the opening was sealed, Flum blew them a kiss.

At the very same moment, one squealed, turned around, and sprayed.

And then they were sealed—except for a small airhole.

The stink!

Sam rubbed at his eyes. It had been a glancing blow, but the young skunk's spray had still got through.

"Oh!" Flum cried.

Gasping, eyes burning, Sam turned on his phone. It provided a dim glow. "Those were skunks, Flum."

He watched understanding flood Flum's watering eyes. "I thought they were kittens."

"I guessed that. No kittens on Osborne?"

They shook their head. "And no skunks."

Sam rubbed his eyes again. "It's okay. It's not too bad."

Flum blinked rapidly. "It's bad!"

"Not as bad as it could have been, trust me."

"I do."

"I am sorry we went to Thyla's house, Flum. I really hoped that we would find something that would help."

Flum repeated what he'd said earlier. "You are very helpful."

Sam decided Flum had made a terrible mistake in putting their faith in him. Sam didn't even have faith in Sam.

Eyes still watering, they returned to tunneling, pushing, wiggling, and making their way. Sam didn't see the point of closing it behind them. Moving the space had the effect of compressing the dirt, making it super strong. Nothing would fall through.

"Are we close?" Flum asked, gasping. They needed air. Good, clean, skunk-free air.

"I don't know." He looked behind them, shone his cell phone light. How far had they come? Were they beyond the park? His shoulders slumped.

What were they doing? It wasn't like they could run forever.

Another very good idea came to him. He activated the map feature on his phone and spoke into the mic: "RCMP detachment."

A squiggle appeared, showing a path from where they were, and ending where Sam wanted to be. "This map will take us to the police."

"Why?"

"We can't keep running, Flum. It will be better if I turn myself in at the detachment. I'll tell them I made a mistake." He put his hand on Flum's shoulder. "It will be okay."

He wished he felt as certain as he sounded.

Telling the authorities the whole truth was impossible. They would never believe him. But what reason would he give them for his breaking in? He looked down at his suit. If he lied and said he wanted to return it, would they take it away? Without the suit he was stuck inside. No. He would simply say that he broke in and that he was sorry. He would say that he couldn't explain why he did it, and that was true.

He would remember to say it respectfully.

He would not mention Flum.

They carried on, until the dirt gave way to cement.

"This is it, Flum. Must be the basement."

It was. They inhaled deeply as they closed the basement wall behind them, then collapsed against metal filing cabinets. It had been hard work to go all that way. Sam turned to Flum. "Whew," he said.

Flum smiled. At least Sam thought they did. His vision shifted. It was like he was watching a livestream video with a wonky feed. He blinked, and Flum was back.

Had he imagined it?

He pressed his hand against his chest where his heart beat a staccato. He'd gotten used to seeing Flum clearly in a sea of cubes. The idea that might change terrified him. He'd come to count on Flum. They'd become his friend.

It was fine. Flum was here, and there was no time to waste.

He pushed back his spaceman hood. "Come on, Flum. Let's face the music." He grinned and explained before Flum could ask. "It's an expression. Stay close, and don't move anything around. I don't know what they'll do if they see something weird."

Flums eyes grew wide.

Light flooded the room. "What in the blazes?" someone asked.

CHAPTER FIFTEEN

JAILHOUSE ROCK

"We have to stop meeting like this," Sam said, then added a "Hehe," so the RCMP officer would know he was joking.

It was the same constable who'd found him exiting Thyla's room. He was holding a stack of files, probably meant for the cabinets he and Flum were now standing beside.

The officer didn't laugh. Instead, he took Sam by the ear and marched him upstairs. So much for turning himself in. He was as caught as caught could get. The door opened to a wide room filled with desks. Immediately there were groans and a slapping of hands over noses.

"Hey, Joe, you forget to wash your socks?"

"Smells like something died down there."

"Strange-looking skunk!"

A sad-looking man with embroidered crowns on his shirt shuffled over and stooped to get a close look at Sam's face. He didn't seem bothered by the smell. "That your fugitive, Joe?"

"It is, Sergeant." Joe puffed out his chest. "We always get our man!"

The sergeant's eyes flicked toward Joe.

Joe looked less puffed. "It's our motto," he said uncertainly.

"No, it isn't."

"I mean it's the Royal Canadian Mounted Police motto."

"No, Joe. It isn't."

"No?"

"It's just something a writer made up a long time ago and it got tossed around TV shows and comic books. Look it up."

There was general chuckling from other officers around the room. The sergeant swung his tired gaze their way. "Can any of you knuckleheads tell us who said it first?"

One by one they shook their heads, cast their eyes back toward their own desks.

"Right," the sergeant said, then looked back to Joe. "Call young Mr. Templeton's father and get him set up in a room."

The only thing Constable Joe said to Sam as he deposited him in a small room with a long table and four chairs was, "You want a soda, kid?"

Sam shook his head.

"Okay, I'll be right back."

Within minutes he returned with a large, clear plastic bag and a package of wet wipes. "I'm assuming you have something on underneath that costume?"

Sam nodded. "It's not a costume. It's a hot suit. Actually, it's called a conductive suit. For lightning protection."

The officer didn't blink. Like everyone else, he'd probably already heard. "Take it off and put it in this bag. We'll keep it for you. It's holding too much of that skunk stink for us to concentrate. You can use the wipes for your face or anywhere else you got sprayed."

"Thank you."

"What I want to know is how you got through our offices and down into our basement without us seeing or smelling you." He quickly held up a hand. "Don't tell me. You can't tell me anything without your dad present. I'm just curious is all."

Sam handed Constable Joe his suit. The room was airconditioned, and he'd only worn a t-shirt and shorts underneath. He shivered in the sudden change from hot and sweaty to chill.

"Hang on," Constable Joe said, and disappeared again. A moment later he was back with a folded RCMP shirt. "This should keep you warm." He handed Sam the shirt and left him alone.

Sam turned to Flum. "Good job on staying quiet," he said. "If I forget and talk to you in front of someone they'll think I'm crazy."

"You're not crazy, Sam. You are the best person I know."

"I'm the only person you know."

"The only Earthling," Flum corrected.

The door opened and Constable Joe stuck his head inside. "You okay, kid?"

"Yes," he said, but this time his eyes strayed to the large mirror beside the door. When Constable Joe closed the door again, Sam turned toward the back of the room and whispered. "It's a two-way mirror, Flum. They're watching us from the other side."

Flum walked up to the mirror and touched their palm to it. "How?"

"It only reflects on this side. On the other side it's a window."

"Oh."

"That means I can't talk to you unless I turn away from it."

"Okay," Flum said. They sat themself in a chair beside Sam and leaned into him. "Your father will be here soon?"

"I hope so."

What if they wanted to put Sam in jail for breaking and entering? That would officially make him a criminal. He felt his armpits begin to sweat, and he wriggled uncomfortably in the shirt that had been so welcome a moment ago.

The door flung open, and Dad rushed inside. "Samuel! Are you okay?"

Sam's heart squeezed at the love and worry that radiated from his father. He swallowed a lump in his throat. "I'm fine. Except I did something stupid."

Flum scooted out of the way just as Dad sat in the chair next to him.

"Tell us about that," Constable Joe said. He'd entered behind Dad, and a female police officer was right behind him.

"I'm Corporal Morrison," the woman said. "Corporal Bell's partner."

"Oh. I thought he was Constable Joe."

Corporal Morrison smiled and looked at her partner.

"I'm a corporal," he said gruffly. He looked like his feelings were hurt.

"Tell you what," the female officer said, "you can call him Corporal Joe if you call me Corporal Sandy."

Sam smiled and nodded. Everything was going to be okay. After all, he hardly fit the picture of a hardened criminal, especially in shorts and t-shirt and a too-big borrowed RCMP shirt.

"Do we need a lawyer?" Dad asked.

"It's your right," Corporal Joe said. "Though I expect this is just a misunderstanding. Mr. and Mrs. Smith aren't pressing charges."

In unison, Sam and Dad breathed a sigh of relief. Flum watched from the end of the table, their nose barely reaching the top.

"They are so nice," Sam said, feeling emotional. "Mrs. Smith already loaned me her suit, and I don't even know if I can get the skunk smell out. I just wish I could see things better."

"Are you confused, Sam?" Corporal Sandy asked gently.

"I mean literally. I wish I could see better with my eyes."

Corporal Joe and Corporal Sandy exchanged a look.

"What's wrong with your eyes, Sam?" Corporal Joe asked as he waved his hand in front of Sam's face.

Dad cleared his throat. "It appears his electrofulguration stimulated unexpected ocular involvement."

The officers blinked.

Corporal Sandy scratched her chin. "Come again?"

Sam saw the subtle shift in his father's face pixels, the tiny pull around his mouth that wasn't quite a smirk. Dad wanted to show the officers he was smarter than them. That meant he was annoyed. Sam had seen and heard his father do this when the phone rang and there was a scammer on the other end trying to tell him there was something wrong with his computer.

"When he was struck by lightning his vision was altered. We expect it will go back to normal when the nerve swelling goes down, but for now, his visualization is pixelated."

Silence from the officers.

"Like I'm in a video game," Sam explained.

"You don't say?" Corporal Joe sounded impressed. "Like *Donkey Kong* and stuff? Like the old games down at Playland?"

He nodded. "It's not so bad once you get used to it. And I can see computer screens like normal."

"Why would—?" Corporal Sandy halted her question when she saw Dad open his mouth to answer. "Never mind that right now. I don't really need to know."

"I'm really sorry about what I did. I only wanted to help." He clamped his mouth shut, but it was too late. He knew what Corporal Sandy's question would be.

"With what?"

Sam swallowed and spoke carefully. "I can't say." Dangerous ground, but he was still telling the truth.

Corporal Joe narrowed his eyes. "You can't, or you won't?"

He was sharper than he looked.

Sam tried again. "I can't explain myself, but I *am* sorry."

Corporal Sandy pursed her lips. "You're very lucky you're not being charged."

"I know that. Can we go now?"

Corporal Joe leaned forward. "What's your hurry, Sam? We're just talking."

Dad stood up abruptly, knocking his chair over in the process. Typical Dad, but to the officers it probably looked like he was making a scene.

"I think we're done here, officers."

"No need to get violent, Mr. Templeton," Corporal Sandy said. She and Corporal Joe also stood.

Dad looked shocked. "Violent?"

Sam didn't like the change in tone this was all taking. He was the only one sitting. The officers and Dad were having a staring contest above him.

"Can I have my suit back?" he squeaked.

Big shiny grins from both RCMP officers. Even without being able to see details, he knew they were fake. The vibrations in the room felt weird. He and Flum exchanged a look. He could tell Flum felt it too.

Corporal Sandy turned back to Sam. "You've been through a lot this week."

"You sure have," said Corporal Joe, but he was still looking at Dad.

They held the door open for Dad and Sam, fake-grinning the whole time. Flum scooted out and fell in beside Sam. Near the front door another officer waited with Sam's suit, still in the plastic bag, a bandana wrapped around her nose. Sam accepted it with a feeling of unease.

Corporal Joe was still standing close to Sam. Too close.

Something was stinky, and it wasn't just the suit.

Dad noticed it too and inserted himself between Corporal Joe and Sam.

Now they were all too close to each other. It was weird and awkward and tense.

Sam stepped back to give his father more room but hadn't noticed that when Dad stepped in front of him, he'd stuck his foot through one handle of the plastic bag. When Sam stepped backward his father must have already been off balance, because his caught leg came out from under him. He fell forward and knocked over Corporal Joe, who fell into someone carrying a stack of papers, which flew up in the air, but it didn't stop there. Shouting told him someone else was bumped, and then another someone else. Sam couldn't see what was happening anymore, only that there was a lot of confused movement and shouting. He felt his father's hand clasp his.

"Let's go, Sam."

Sam, Dad and Flum hurried away from the chaos.

CHAPTER SIXTEEN

THE WHOLE TRUTH

Faced with putting the suit back on with full stink, or going outside without it, Sam chose the suit and quickly dressed. He wasn't ready to face what he'd gone through when he'd tried to go outside without it. He glanced at Flum. So much had changed in just a few days.

Dad didn't complain about the smell. He didn't say anything at all, which Sam found strange. It wasn't like he expected him to blow up or anything—he wasn't a blow-up kind of person. But Sam had clearly done something stupid, wrong, *and* illegal. Any father worth his cookies should have something to say about it, and Dad was worth a lot.

"Um," Sam began, "should we talk about this?"

His father nodded. "Yes, absolutely." He cleared his throat. "We will." He continued to nod, like he couldn't stop, like he was suddenly a Dad bobblehead doll. "Couple of stops first."

Sam shifted in his seat and made more room for Flum, who was sandwiched next to the window. *Something feels wrong,* he thought. Wrong in a different way than how his world had been turned inside out and bizzaro.

Dad parked by the Ready Mart. "Wait here," he said. A moment later he was back, carrying a large paper grocery bag. Two blocks farther, he stopped in front of the Sudsy Laundry Barn and turned to Sam. "Come inside with me."

Their washing machine had kicked the bucket when Sam was eight. Dad said they didn't need a machine of their own, and since then every Friday he'd drop off their weekly bag of laundry. Every Monday he'd pick it up. Mr. Pockets, the owner, was surprised Dad didn't have a full bag of clothes with him today. If he was also surprised by Sam's skunk smell, he didn't say so. There were lots of campgrounds close by. Maybe he was used to it.

"Bit of an emergency," Dad said. He set the four big cans of tomato juice he'd bought on the counter while Sam stripped off his suit. "Can we put this in your machine?"

Mr. Pockets took the suit from Dad and set it next to the cans. "I'll take care of it for you."

"I can't ask you to do that, Bill. It's kind of terrible."

"Not so bad. You should see some of what comes in here. I insist. Hour and a half."

Sam didn't want to think about the other laundry emergencies Mr. Pockets had seen. What could be worse than skunk?

"Thank you, Bill. We'll wait in your movie room."

Mr. Pockets winked at Sam. "Just got the latest *Pinky Parks* in. In this one Pinky goes to Texas to rescue a valuable Gilla Monster."

Sam had outgrown *Pinky Park*s years ago but thanked Mr. Pockets anyway. Some grownups had no sense of what kids liked at different ages. "Sounds like a good one," he said.

Mr. Pockets smiled big teeth cubes and handed Sam a lollipop. Flum's eyes grew wide. Was there candy on their world?

Sam cried out as Flum suddenly disappeared.

"Samuel?" Dad reached out to him.

A bunch of dots appeared and zig-zagged as if they were chasing each other, and then Flum was back. Solid. No dots.

"Don't like strawberry?" Mr. Pockets asked. "You can have grape."

"Uh, no, this is good, thanks." He stuck it in his pocket. "I just remembered something. All of a sudden, like."

Dad tilted his head. "What?"

"I, ah…I left the water running. In the bathtub."

"No, you didn't."

"I didn't?"

"No."

"What a relief, hehe!"

A vertical crease appeared between Dad's eyebrow cubes as they smashed together. He pressed a hand on Sam's shoulder. "Let's sit down."

"Hour and a half!" Mr. Pockets said again, then disappeared into the back of his shop.

Dad chose an old Iron Man movie, but it was clear by the way he turned his back to it and pulled his chair in front of Sam's that he had no intention of watching. Still, it gave Sam something to see with clear vision other than Flum, who'd settled cross-legged on the floor to watch the movie.

"Want to tell me what's going on, son?"

Hiding things was making his head hurt. He shrugged. "I wish I could tell you."

"That's an interesting answer, Samuel. Just like when

you told the RCMP officers that you couldn't explain. You *can* tell me, and you *can* explain. You are choosing not to, and I'd like to know why."

The silence that followed made Sam squirm. His father knew him too well. Sam also knew his father. This was Dad waiting for Sam to spill.

But he couldn't. He wanted to, but—

He glanced again at Flum. It was too impossible.

"I'm sorry. I can't tell you either."

Dad dropped his chin to his chest and sighed. He looked up again and took Sam's hand in his. "Son, I know I haven't been quite myself lately, but we've always been able to talk." He chewed on his bottom lip, like he always did when he was thinking. "Let's come at this another way. What would you like to hear from me?"

Sam's heart leapt. Dad probably meant regarding the current circumstances, but it was also the opening he'd been looking for. It was an invitation to ask his biggest question.

He opened his mouth to say all of this, but nothing came out. He looked at Flum, searching for the right words.

Then he had them.

"Where have you been? I mean, in your head. Sometimes we are in the same room but it's like you're somewhere else."

If Dad was surprised, he didn't show it. Instead, he nodded as if he'd been expecting this. "I've been thinking a lot about your mother."

"I get it. I mean, that Icelandic database has interesting stuff that led me to other stuff I can't even—" he was about to tell him about the werewolf guy but stopped when he noticed the pain in his father's face.

The part that shook him was that he could see it clear. No pixels! Just like when Flum faded, it only lasted a blink before the pixels returned.

"That's true, Samuel, but it's not because of the database. She been on my mind for months now."

The pixel weirdness could wait. He was about to learn everything he'd wanted to know.

"I understood what you were trying to tell me with your experiment, and it was wrong for me to not acknowledge that. I guess I just didn't know how."

Sam felt warmth flood through him. This was going to be even better than he'd hoped. They were talking—really talking! The bug bomb of honesty had been deployed. They would right whatever had gone wrong and would get back to normal. He glanced once more at Flum. As normal as possible. "I'm pretty sure you know everything," he said.

Dad grinned. "Not everything, and I'm not good with discussing my emotions." He sighed. "That's what your mother used to say, but I never really understood what she meant." He got quiet. "I wonder sometimes if that's why she left."

Sam didn't know what to say. He had no memory of Dory to make Dad feel better.

"You remind me so much of her. You look like her and sound like her."

"You said I have the same enthusiasm."

"Yes, that too. You were born on the winter solstice. Did you know that?"

He shook his head. He knew that his birthday was always near the darkest time of the year because Derek always teased him about it, but he never really thought about it.

"The winter solstice marks the shortest day of the year before days begin to get longer. Your mother said in old times, Icelanders celebrated the winter solstice as the rebirth of the sun. To her it was extra special that it was also your birthday. Rebirth of the ball of gas sun, and birth of our son. You."

"But the solstice isn't always on the same day. I remember that from science class."

Dad looked pleased. "That's right. In your lifetime it has been December 22nd twice. The year you were born, and again last year." Dad looked like he was seeing someplace far away. "The solstice made me think of her even more than I usually do, and when you turned twelve it hit me that you were growing up. I could see it. I can see *her* in you. It scared me, because I realized that one day, you'll leave me too."

"No, I won't."

"Not completely. But you'll have your own life."

"I'm only twelve!"

Dad laughed. "Going on thirteen. I can see now it was just a bunch of worry and fretting that would probably have gone away if we'd talked about it. Instead, I let those feelings stew. I got lost in remembering your mother."

"She shouldn't have stayed away," Sam said. "We're her family."

Dad looked sadly at him. "She loved you so much." He reached over, squeezed his hand. "And I love you, more than anything."

"More than science?"

"Definitely more than science."

"But you really like science."

"I really do."

Sam looked at Flum, who was intent on the movie.

"That's good, because I need to tell you something that some people would think is magic, but I think is science that we haven't learned about yet." He knew Dad would appreciate the science part, and that he thought that way.

Dad looked confused, and a little worried. "What's going on, Samuel?"

Sam took a deep breath. It was now or never. "I can see in between pixels."

Dad's eyebrows went up.

"And I can move them. The pixels."

Dad's eyebrows went way up.

"Look." Sam tapped Flum's shoulder to get their attention, shifted in his chair, and tapped along the edge of it. Flum understood and tapped as well. Sam then wiggled and shifted until one edge of the seat looked slightly longer.

He expected Dad to be shocked. Instead, he calmly crouched beside the chair, peered at it, took out a pencil and marked it. "Can you move it back?"

He did. Dad sat back down in his chair.

The silence got loud.

"So?" he asked.

Dad swallowed audibly. "Quantum physics isn't my area of study."

"So there is a scientific explanation?"

"Yes," he said. But he didn't sound sure. "Yes," he said again, more firmly. "Several years ago two scientists won a Nobel prize for particle manipulation."

Dad began to vibrate, just as he had when talking to his friend Dr. Engel about getting back into his research. He loved this stuff!

"Particle manipulation. Is that what I'm doing?"

"My notes on it are at home. Wait." He pulled out his phone and began tapping. "Here," he said, and handed it to Sam. It was a webpage describing how scientists Serge Haroche and David J. Wineland learned how to trap ions and control them with photons, plus a bunch of other stuff Sam didn't understand.

"Photons. Like in *Star Trek*?"

"The photon torpedoes in *Star Trek* are made up, but they are rooted in science. Photons are particles that carry electromagnetic radiation." The vibration coming off his father now was so strong Sam could see it, like a halo of tiny, glowing blocks shifting and moving around his head. "Something must have happened within your molecular structure when you were struck by lightning."

A metallic tapping sound drew his attention to the television. It was the scene where Iron Man first puts on his suit.

Dad followed Sam's gaze. "There is a reason so many fictional superheroes are struck by lightning."

Sam laughed. "So I'm a superhero?"

"You're real, Samuel." Dad took his hand. "This is incredible, and we're going to study it while we can."

"What do you mean?"

"According to the tests we did, there is no lasting damage to your system. Remember? You will return to normal. Until then, what you are going through might be an incredible boost to our scientific community. Tell me everything. Don't leave anything out."

Sam gulped. Even though he'd wanted Dad to get back into his research, he couldn't help feeling like something growing in a petri dish. But he'd already gone this far, and Dad might be able to help. "There is one more thing." Two more, if he added Thyla. But he'd already gone down that road with Dad. One impossible thing at a time.

"What is it, son?"

"You'll think I'm crazy."

"I haven't yet."

True. He reached into his pocket for the lollipop and handed it to Flum.

He didn't know for sure what his father was seeing, but he guessed it would be a stick floating in the air as the candy disappeared in Flum's mouth.

Dad stared; his mouth open wide.

"It's Flum," Sam said. "They came through a shift that the lightning opened up. Maybe. Pretty sure."

"I don't—"

Sam waited, remembering his own confusion when he first encountered Flum.

"I don't—"

Sam waited some more.

Dad's brows smashed together. "Are you doing this? Are you somehow...are you—?"

Sam had never seen his father so at a loss for words. "It's not me, Dad." He spotted a towel on a nearby clothes dryer, borrowed it and draped it over Flum so that some of their shape appeared. "Flum."

"Plum?" Dad's voice was faint.

"Flum," Sam corrected. "Don't worry, you're not crazy. I thought the same thing at first. They're from an alternate world called Osborne. They know about lots of alternate worlds."

Dad took a deep breath, exhaled, and began muttering super fast. "Quantum physics. More quantum physics. It-it-it's okay. It's okay."

Flum stuck out their thumb. "May all be very well," they said to Dad.

Sam repeated the greeting to Dad, and then guided his thumb to shake Flum's.

"And…also with you," Dad choked out.

The sound of singing came from the other room. Mr. Pockets. Sam removed the towel. Just as it was important for Dad to know, it was also important that no one else did.

"Except something is changing," he said.

"What do you mean?" Dad and Flum said together.

"When we got here, when Mr. Pockets gave me the candy, Flum disappeared for a second. But it started before that, after we went through the dirt tunnel—"

"Wait, what?"

"We were running from the police and had to tunnel to the station," Sam explained. He got the feeling Dad's head might explode. "Sorry, there's lots more to tell."

Dad's mouth was hanging open again. "Go on."

"After the tunnel, they faded for a second, and then when Mr. Pockets gave me the sucker, they blipped right out and then came back."

"That's why you shouted."

"Yes. And a few minutes ago I saw you clearly. Without the pixels, and then the pixels came back."

"But you have to see me!" Flum pleaded. "You are the only one! If you don't see me and we can't see together, how will I get home?"

"Don't worry, Flum. Dad can help." He turned back to his father, who was glancing wildly between Sam and the chair beside him. "Flum and I have been trying to find a doorway that came apart when they got here."

"Doorway?"

"It's called a shift, and it's the way between alternate worlds. It broke in pieces during the lightning strike." He motioned for Flum to pull out the shard. They did. "This is a piece of it."

After Dad had a good look, Flum tucked it away. Dad blinked rapidly.

A bell tinkled and the door of the Sudsy opened. It was Corporal Joe and Corporal Sandy. Their eyes locked on Dad.

"Gordon Templeton, we need you to come with us."

Dad's brows mashed together. "I don't understand. Why?"

"You are under arrest for assaulting an RCMP officer."

CHAPTER SEVENTEEN

ALAKAZAM!

Murphy's Law, which was not a legal law nor a scientific principle but nevertheless true, stated: Whatever can go wrong, will.

When corporals Sandy and Joe arrived at the Sudsy to arrest Dad for the chain reaction that happened at the RCMP detachment, things went from bad to worse. Sam had just told his father what was likely the most incredible mind-blowing thing he'd heard in his entire life. He didn't take well to being interrupted before he could ask Sam a billion questions.

"No!" he'd shouted, jumped to his feet, and knocked over a coffee table.

"More violence, Mr. Templeton?" Corporal Joe asked as he took out a pair of handcuffs.

Mr. Pockets emerged from the back room just in time to see Dad attempting to push away the handcuffs. Instead, he accidentally socked Corporal Joe in the nose. Now his father and a lawyer were in an interrogation room with Corporal Sandy and Corporal Joe, while Sam and Flum sat on a wooden bench in the hall with a social worker named Bayland Rader.

Bayland didn't look much older than Thyla, which meant he probably whizzed through school super fast and graduated super young. Sam was doomed to live his life surrounded by geniuses. It wasn't that he was dumb. He was normal. But next to Dad and Thyla, and now Bayland Rader, Sam felt like he had the IQ of a banana.

Down the hall, an RCMP officer with a stack of files piled higher than his head missed an open doorway, smashed into the wall next to it, and dropped the files. Sam felt comfort in this. People were people and smacked into walls no matter their IQ. Sam had done it, but so had Dad. He'd even seen Thyla do it. She'd been walking along the sidewalk, reading, and ran right into a telephone pole. Rather than being embarrassed about it, she'd laughed, waved at Sam, and tucked her book in her bag.

Maybe smart people didn't get embarrassed by things like that.

Sam did stupid things all the time. Breaking into the Smiths' house was just one more. A big one. In doing that big, stupid thing he'd messed things up royally, especially for Dad.

He wished he could wish it away. This whole mess had begun with Monday's lightning strike. If only he hadn't gone to the park that day. He could have just stayed in. If he never went outside again, there would be considerably less chance of crazy accidents and his doing stupid things.

Except that he didn't want to be someone who lived life afraid of things that might never happen. Sam knew he wasn't going to be struck by lightning every time he went outside. He understood it would likely never happen again.

Knowing something in your head and convincing your body of the same wasn't easy.

He sighed. At least he had his suit.

Bayland stood and held out his hand. "I have to take that suit."

His insides clenched. "Where?"

"Don't worry. I'll keep it safe." He gave him an admonishing look. "You can't sit there soaking wet. I'll look for a spot to hang it up, give it a chance to dry."

At the Sudsy, Sam had put the suit back on wet rather than go outside without it. It still smelled like skunk and was now stained blotchy red from the juice.

Sam stripped off the suit and shivered. Bayland handed him a thin, blue blanket, grimaced, and stuffed the suit in a bag. He disappeared down the hall and returned five minutes later.

"When can we go home?" Sam asked.

"There is news. Your father will be kept overnight."

"But he didn't do anything!"

"A process is in place."

When Sam didn't respond, Bayland sighed noisily as if Sam should know all this. "Your father has been arrested. He will be arraigned in the morning and bail will be set."

A fluttering started in Sam's stomach. "Let me talk to the police again. This is all my fault. All Dad did was—"

Bayland held his hand up. "Your father has a lawyer to look after him. I am a social worker. I am here for you, not your father."

"But—"

"Enough. It's time for us to go."

A soft buzzing began in Sam's head. This wasn't fair. It was entirely *un*fair.

"Come on, Sam. Your foster is waiting."

"Wait, what?"

"We've placed you in an emergency foster home for tonight, possibly a few nights, depending on what happens in court tomorrow."

Sam's voice rose. "A *few* nights?" Like he'd been pricked by a pin, all the air fizzled out of him. He leaned back and tried to imagine how his dad felt. Sam was scared. Was Dad scared too?

"Let's go," Bayland Rader said.

The social worker looked immovable, but there was still a chance Sam could get them out of this. A small one. If everything worked just right. "I can't go anywhere without my suit."

"It's filthy."

"You don't understand. I have a condition."

Bayland Rader looked at his clipboard. "I don't see anything."

"It's new. I'm afraid to go outside without it." Bayland Rader didn't look convinced. Sam added, "I was hit by lightning."

"Oh. You're that kid?"

Sam nodded.

The social worked sighed again, but softer. "Okay. Wait here while I get your suit and some paper towels. I don't want it messing up my car."

Bayland Rader walked smartly down the hall.

"What are we going to do now?" Flum asked. They faded, then came back. At least they didn't blip out completely, like at the Sudsy.

"We have to break him out, Flum. Now, while we're alone."

Flum looked shocked. "That would be wrong!"

"It's our only chance."

"When we were in the dirt, you decided to come here even though you knew it would be complicated. You were right to do that."

"Flum, you don't understand—"

"I do. You are worried about your father. Did he do wrong?"

"No, but—"

"Then you must wait and trust this will be revealed. It is important to do right, Sam." As Flum patted Sam's knee, their hand faded in and out.

"Flum, you're fading," Sam whispered. "We don't have much time."

What he could still see of Flum's blue skin paled.

"Dad and I will come back to the detachment later. It isn't like we're going to fly off to Iceland and disappear." He swallowed. He and Dad were both thinking a lot about Dory lately.

"Ice land? Like Baffinalt?"

"Not exactly. Together, we have powers, but they may not last long. Dad knows science. He can help us. He can help you! We need to act now and face the music later."

"Music?"

"Another expression, Flum!" He was getting irritated. Flum was only trying to understand, but the urgency was driving Sam out of his mind. He took a breath and forced calm into his voice. "We need to do this before it's too late for you."

Flum nodded solemnly as they considered, then sprang from their seat. "Let's get him out."

"Great!" Sam looked at the door. If it was locked, they

could wiggle it open. They could also wiggle open the wall, but with corporals Sandy and Joe inside Sam didn't think they would win if they got into a Dad tug-of-war.

Just then the interrogation room door opened and the two RCMP officers stepped into the hall. They glanced his way with serious eyes, then headed in the same direction that the social worker had disappeared into.

What a break!

The buzzing in his head moved into his whole body. It was like the soft jolt from joining palms with Flum was spreading all the way through him. He felt like Iron Man! No, he felt like Iron Man's suit.

Time to move!

Sam dropped the blanket and pulled Flum with him to the door. It would be locked, but they could fix that. They twined thumbs and reached for the knob. To his shock, their hands went right through, followed by their bodies. It was like pushing through air! He looked at Flum. "That was weird."

On the other side, shocked silence from Dad and his lawyer. The lawyer fainted.

"Samuel?" Dad croaked.

"We have to go!"

He expected his father to argue, instead, he checked the lawyer's pulse. "I don't think we should be here when he wakes up." He glanced at Sam. "I'm not saying it's right to run away. I just—We need to figure out the science. History shows the misunderstood are not given the benefit of time."

Voices in the hall. The corporals were coming back—or the social worker, or maybe all of them. It wouldn't take long to guess that Sam came in here.

"Take my hand!" he said to his father, holding firm to Flum with his other. "I'm not sure if this will work." He took a breath and pushed through the wall into the next room. "Whew!" he said, after confirming Flum and Dad were with him. And also because the room was empty.

"This may go beyond particle manipulation," Dad squeaked.

They pushed into the next room where they weren't so lucky. There was a dazed-looking man cuffed to a chair. Maybe he was waiting to be questioned, or maybe RCMP officers on the other side of the two-way mirror were getting an eyeful.

The man rubbed his eyes with balled-up fists, then looked the other way and began to whistle. It was as if he'd decided they didn't exist.

"Hello?" Sam said.

The man whistled louder.

Assuming he couldn't see Flum, he would still have seen a boy and a man appear like magic before him. He clearly didn't believe his eyes. Nor his ears.

There was one shout joined by more shouts from the room they'd just vacated. "They know we're gone," Dad said.

Sam didn't want to risk going through another wall without knowing who or what might be waiting for them. Instead, he let go of Dad and Flum, carefully opened the door, and poked his head into the hallway. Empty! "Come on," Sam whispered. "If we walk slow and normal, no one will notice us."

He stuck his hands in his pockets and assumed a stroll. One step, two steps, tens steps. So far so good. Sam almost felt like whistling. *Nothing to see here, folks!*

"Stop!" It was Corporal Sandy.

They did not.

There was complete and sudden chaos as they sprinted through the central office and snaked around cabinets. Beside a leafy plant, they were suddenly blocked by a burly officer. Sam's sneakers squeaked as he stopped and pivoted. It was like cat and mouse. Pretty soon they had officers running in every direction as they tried to catch them.

Abruptly, they found themselves in front of the basement door. Sam pulled it open, and they clattered down the stairs.

"I don't think this is the right way," Dad said.

"Trust me! Keep running!"

They were down and around the corner when the sound of many heavy feet hit the stairs.

There! The tall filing cabinets.

"Come on!"

Flum and Sam each grabbed hold of one of Dad's hands, and they were through.

Silence.

Darkness.

Breathing.

And muffled shouts from the other side of the wall. But they were safe. For now. Chest heaving, Sam turned on his phone for light. He saw Dad's eyes were glassy. Something else. Sam saw his father with regular vision, not pixelated. Sam moved his hand into the phone's glow. Normal!

His vision had returned.

"Dad, I can see!" Then, a terrible, horrible realization scissored through him. He looked frantically into the shadows. "Flum?" He cast the dim beam of the phone all around.

His friend was gone.

"Flum, I can't see you!"

"He's...here." Dad lifted his hand, fingers curled as if he held hands with someone.

"They're here," Sam corrected.

"Pardon?"

"Osbornians are one gender." Sam heard soft sobbing, which grew into a wail. "Hush, Flum." Sam reached to pat where he imagined their shoulder would be. There it was. "It's okay. I can still hear and feel you. You're only invisible to my eyes."

Sam fell backward as Flum flung their arms around him in a hug. "Oh good," Flum cried. "I thought, I thought—"

"It's okay," Sam said again, holding his palm up for Flum's touch. There it was—the jolt. Soft, but there. Why was the jolt soft? He patted Flum's shoulder again to reassure himself. Still solid, and very much there, but the electrical connection with the touch thing was fading. He turned to his father. "It's not too late."

"Tell me, Samuel. Tell me everything. "Dad glanced at the wall. The shouting hadn't stopped. "You can explain as we move."

It wasn't likely the RCMP officers would think they'd vaporized through the basement foundation, but it was getting stuffy in the tunnel. More importantly, he didn't know how long they had before he would no longer hear Flum, or how long the special power they had together would last.

As they rushed through the tunnel, he told his father everything Flum had explained about alternates and shifts, and how Flum had discovered this new shift at the same time Sam was struck by lightning. "We found one shard in the park, but we need to find all of them, and fast. If Flum and I lose our connection, this thing we can do together won't work."

Dad stopped and leaned against the tunnel wall. His eyes closed and Sam watched his eyeballs twitching beneath their lids, is if they were mechanical. In a way they were. Dad's brain machine at its finest! Finally, they opened. "I suspect that use of your new and very unusual abilities has acted as extra stimulation on those parts of your brain that were affected by the electromagnetic pulses from the lightning. It has had the effect of therapy. In essence, the exercise has sped healing."

"But it can't heal!" Sam and Flum said together.

"Of course it can. The brain has a remarkable ability to heal itself in ways that we don't yet fully understand."

"It can't heal *yet*," Sam clarified. "Not until we find the shards from Flum's shift."

"Then we'd best hurry."

They dashed as fast as they could with the dim beam of Sam's phone to show the way. Dad ran bent at the waist and tried not to scrape his head against the top.

"The officers have no reason to believe we will be in the park" he puffed, "but it won't take long to search the village. Tell me quick how this works."

"We looked through my camera. We looked and didn't look until we saw the pieces."

"I don't understand."

"Like a magic eye puzzle."

"Ah. I never could do those." He added an "Ow!" as his head hit a protruding root.

"We used the camera because of my crazy eyes and so that we could look together. It was the only way I could see clear."

"So hold hands and look but don't look. With your vision restored you won't need your camera, which should speed up your search."

Sam felt Flum squeeze his hand.

The end of the tunnel appeared faster than their eyes could register, and they smacked into the end-dirt with an "Oof," "Oof," and "Oof." Dad rubbed his head and tapped at the dirt ceiling. "You sure this is where you came through?"

"Yes." He touched the dirt. "Here's our air hole."

"It's like cement."

Sam cast a furtive glance around the compact space. They had nothing to use to break through, not even an errant rock. When they'd compressed the space, every loose stone had been embedded.

"We need a boost," Flum said.

Sam smiled. "Dad, Flum and I will climb on your back and if our powers still work, we will go through like we did at the police station. Then we'll reach back in for you. I think between the two of us we will be able to pull you up."

"Samuel, manipulating particles in any way may speed your healing further."

Sam exhaled. He had no other ideas.

Flum's voice was muffled, as if speaking through cotton. "We have no choice."

Sam nodded agreement.

Dad glanced back the way they'd come. "Okay. Let's try it." He got down on his knees and braced himself like a table. Sam and Flum balanced carefully on his back.

Flum joined their hand with Sam's. "Ready," they said.

They pushed through.

The dirt layer was thicker than Sam remembered, and

he feared they might get stuck. They would drown in dirt! Then he felt a lift. His father rose like an elevator.

They were through!

Now for Dad.

"Reach!" Sam cried. They pushed their arms as far as they could back into the dirt. Except now there was resistance. Dirt was in the way!

Their power was fading.

Sam let go of Flum and spun to find something he could use to dig into the ground. He saw three tiny black and white tails raised toward him.

"N—" he didn't even get the word out before he was sprayed. Triple whammy. So much worse than before! Coughing, gasping, choking, he rubbed at his eyes and flung himself away seeking air, any air. He scraped his palms over the rough wooden slats that made up the inside of the boat-slide hull, found cool ground at its base, and a few blades of grass. He pulled up a handful of dirt and grass, spat on it, and instinctively rubbed the mash against his eyes.

Relief. His eyes stopped watering and he was able to see, though the air was still awful.

It was quiet. He realized the only coughing he'd heard was his own.

"Flum?"

Nothing.

"Flum!" he wailed.

"Sam?" Dad's voice was faint through the air hole. "Are you okay?"

Curling himself into a ball he held his knees. He rocked and softly wept, which helped the sting in his eyes.

The skunks decided he wasn't a threat after all and played tag in the corner.

He wiped his eyes and looked around. It was like a great Flum-shaped hole had opened inside of him. But he couldn't stop, not now. Dad was still trapped in the tunnel.

He looked about. There were no tools. There! Next to the skunks he spied a small chunk of cement.

"Nice skunkies," he cooed as he reached for it. The skunks couldn't appear to care less as they tumbled one over the other in an apparent wrestling match.

Sam rushed to where he and Flum had come through, looked around, wondered if Flum was watching him, or if they were upset and sobbing as they had been when Sam first found them, worried they might never get home. "Flum, I know you are here, even though I can't see or hear you. I just want you to know, you're my friend." Sam's eyes flooded once more. "You will always be my friend." Silently he added, *I'm sorry I failed you.*

He swallowed and began whacking at the air hole, then pushing, pushing. It was working. He broke up the dirt while the young skunks sat all in a row, watching him like curious kittens. He cupped his hands and scooped away the crumbled dirt until he was stopped by something firm.

It was the ceiling of the tunnel, hard as cement. When he and Flum made the tunnel, the dirt had nowhere to go. When they'd pushed and made space, they'd compacted it.

"I'm sorry, Dad," he sobbed. "I failed you too."

An itch on his back flared so insistent that he had to scratch. It didn't help. The one itch became a wave, as if a million tiny ants raced up and down his back. When he thought he could bear it no longer, it soothed to a vibration that moved into his arm, to his hand, and into his fingers. He felt a gentle and familiar pulse. "Flum? Is that you?"

The sensation was soft, but there. It was a chance.

Like in the beginning, when they first learned they could manipulate pixels and therefore particles, Sam pushed and wiggled and pried. "It's working!"

Sam's hands pulsed and he pried some more. They broke through! Dad grinned and gave a relieved thumbs up. They continued working until the space was wide enough to climb through. Dad stood fully upright in the hole and poked his head up over the edge.

"Samuel! You had me worried there. Stand clear." There were a few grunts and puffs. "It's. Not. That. High," Dad puffed as he jumped. Finally, he locked both arms and elbows above the hole. He gasped and grunted some more, rolled up and over the edge, then lay flat in the dirt, still puffing. "Guess I'm not in shape like I used to be."

"Dad, I can't hear Flum. And I can't see them. I think they helped me open the dirt, but I don't know for sure." He felt his knees wobble. "It's like it was only my weird eyes that made him real." Sam felt like his brain was a wind-up top that would never stop spinning. "How is that possible? How is any of this possible?"

"They're still here," Dad said, his voice steady.

Sam wiped sweaty palms against his pants and listened. All he could hear was the thump of his own heart. "Are you sure?"

"Yes. We knew this might happen. Just because your senses no longer register their presence, this doesn't mean they're gone. From what we understand, Flum is still here, and they need you."

"What can I do?"

"You can try. Like you always do."

Like Dory, Sam thought.

He felt warmth spark in his belly. "I will. I'll find a way, even if I am normal again."

Dad chuckled. "I'm not sure Team Templeton will ever be normal." He stopped laughing and looked serious. "I'm sorry, Samuel. This is no time to joke."

"I didn't know you could joke. Not until Dr. Engel said so."

Dad smiled. "Let's see what we can do."

"What if making a door out of here uses up the last of our power?"

Dad stood up as best he could under the low ceiling, brushed off the dirt and moved to the side of the hull. The skunks followed him all in a row, but it was like Dad didn't even see them. He hadn't even commented on the stink.

"Ah, here it is." With a soft click, he pulled open a hatch door. "It's well hidden so kids don't find it, but park workers need to get in here from time to time to clear out skunks and whatnot." He held the hatch open, and the skunklets walked out, one, two, three.

"Is it always that easy?"

"Nope. Come on."

On hands and knees, they crawled through. Thankfully, the park was empty. Sam's growling stomach suggested that the kids who were playing here earlier had likely gone home for dinner. They sprinted toward where the lamppost used to be and stopped short. "Oh no!" Sam cried.

The pattern was gone. Trampled into nothing.

CHAPTER EIGHTEEN

NO PLACE LIKE HOME

"Looks like someone played soccer overtop of it," Dad said. "Everyone knows about your accident. I think the outside world finally found us. I followed a chartered bus on my way back from the city earlier. They must have come to look at the pattern."

"And wrecked it," Sam said.

Dad pointed to the park trash basket overfull with candy wrappers and a flyer. Sam could just make out the headline: "Daytrip to site of miracle boy lightning survival. $10."

Great.

He heard a low rumble and looked up. A storm! A regular one, with black-bottomed clouds that pushed and slotted together like a jigsaw puzzle. His blood ran cold. "My suit. Dad, I don't have my suit!" Bayland Rader had taken it to dry. That was the last he'd seen of it.

He flung himself at his father, his breath coming in shallow gasps.

"It's okay, Samuel. It's okay."

"No," he gulped. "It isn't. I don't have my suit, and the pattern is almost gone."

"It's okay, Samuel. I'll help. We'll find it."

"You don't understand! The shards are in the pattern. If we can't see the pattern—" He couldn't say it. It was too awful. He tried to imagine what it must be like for Flum, to see this and know all hope was lost. He was stuck here, alone and far from home. Maybe forever.

He felt a fluttery vibration on his back. It was different from before. It felt like the pat of a hand. A touch from a source you couldn't see felt different from one where you could see the source. It was like his brain wanted to convince him it was something else, but he knew.

"Flum?" He waited, felt it again, and turned to his father. "I think Flum is trying to make me feel better." That was so like them.

He felt the vibration again, and then it came in pulses. Almost smacks. They were smacks!

"Hey, are you hitting me?" Then he got it. Flum was trying to tell him something. "Dad, my back!"

Dad helped Sam remove his shirt. He took Sam's phone to snap a photo. "You sure it's the same as what you saw on the ground?"

"I'm sure!" He held the phone out. "Flum, I know you can see this. You're right. We can use the picture of my back to find the shards."

Dad peered closer at the screen. "Where did you find the first shard?"

As he looked around, the fear of being in the wide open with a storm moving in nearly knocked him to the ground. *Breathe!* He told himself. *Just breathe!*

He felt his pulse slow. He felt Dad rubbing his back. He also felt a pulse on his fingers. *Flum.* It was faint, but this thing they had together wasn't completely gone. He sat up, swallowed, and imagined pushing his anxiety back down into his gut where it shrivelled into a tiny pea.

He could do this.

He looked again at the photo and brought it close. There was something weird about it, something he hadn't noticed before. He held it out for Dad—and maybe Flum—to see. "Look! There is a pattern inside the pattern, dark parts on my back where it's starting to heal. Do you see it?"

"Is that…?"

"You see it too!" He turned to where he thought Flum might be. "It's the design on my mother's stone tray. And my blanket."

"Same as on the old piano bench," Dad said. "Which we don't have anymore."

"The old Icelandic stave for protection. The Helm of Awe."

Dad frowned. "The same pattern on your back as on the ground is one thing, possibly explained by electromagnetic mirroring, but these other things, these connections to your mother." His eyes blinked fast. "I don't understand the science."

Sam squeezed his dad's hand. "Let's worry about that later."

Using the phone, they matched where the branches of the pattern had once been visible, and then Dad dragged his foot to make a perfect match of the darker etchings on Sam's back until his mother's magical symbol was clearly visible. Out the corner of his eye, looking and not looking, Sam saw a glimmer of light. And then another, slightly brighter along a different part of the stave.

"I think it's working!" he cried.

A flash revealed a shard, and then three more, until they'd found them all. They placed the shards all together and waited.

Nothing.

No doorway to another world appeared.

Sam's heart sank into the soles of his feet. All their effort had been in vain. It had not been enough. Sam had not been enough. He had failed his friend.

The thunder boomed louder now, and a fat drop of rain hit his upturned face, shooting another jolt of fear through his body. In the distance, he heard a siren. He and Dad turned toward it. It grew louder. More drops now.

Another siren joined the first.

"They're coming, Dad. They know we're here."

"It's okay. Keep looking. Maybe we missed something."

It got worse. The rain now came in sheets and obscured the ground.

"No!" Sam cried as he ran into the centre of the churned-up grass and mud. Dirty water pooled as the rain came so hard it stung his face and bounced off the surface.

He saw a shape in the rain, like tear drop, with a wide bottom and a torso that narrowed toward its large head. Its legs were short, and its feet long. Its arms ran nearly its whole length. "Flum!"

His panic blipped away, like a candle snuffed.

He felt a new vibration, in the ground and moving up all the way from his toes to his knees. It was the same as he'd felt Monday afternoon.

"Oh, no," he gasped. "Not again."

Instinctively, he dropped to the ground and curled in

a ball. There was a buzz, a click, and a hissing sound, like static. He waited for the bang, but it didn't come.

Instead, everything hushed and the world around him—trees and flowers, the slide, the Free Little Library—began to glow around the edges. It was like auras Sam had read about, except they touched everything, living and not. The rain stopped. The sirens stopped. The park faded away and he was in a long cavern with walls of silvery, shimmery fog that reached high, high toward a blanket of ink and stars. Within the cavern walls, there was a thin mist. Far ahead, a wall of bright light moved closer.

It was as if the Earth's atmosphere had peeled away, and he and Dad might touch the universe. He looked at his father to make sure he was seeing it too, that this wasn't another weird gift from his accident. Dad was wide-eyed and pale. He was definitely seeing it.

Sam felt Flum's hand on his arm. He blinked back tears. "This is it, isn't it? The shift."

The vibration wrapped around him like a hug. It was a hug. He hugged back. "I'm happy for you, Flum," he said, tears streaming. "I'll miss you."

Like a whisper inside his head he heard, *May all be very well.*

He reached for his father, who clasped his hand as Flum walked away. He felt empty, but full. He watched and waited for the Flum-shaped space in the rain and mist to disappear into the light.

The wall of light stopped, as if also waiting. Sam's special vision was gone, but he saw enough. He could make out the vague shape of Flum as they moved the mist on their way toward the wall.

They stopped. They moved one way and then another, as if blocked. A dark line appeared and stretched between Flum and the wall. For a reason Sam couldn't fathom, Flum did not cross.

Did not, or could not?

Another movement drew Sam's eye upward. One of the stars became a dot of glowing blue. It grew larger as it sank toward them until it took the shape of a blue jellyfish. It was called a *sprite*, he remembered. At least that was the name for the phenomena he'd seen when struck by lightning. That one had been red. The blue jellyfish lowered until it hovered before the black line. It shimmered and began to change. Sam watched as the jellyfish morphed into the hazy shape of a woman. Beside her, the Flum shape in the rain and mist became more solid until they were once again fully visible.

Sam heard a gasp and glanced at his father just in time to see him faint.

Samuel.

The voice spoke in the air between him, and also inside his head. It was familiar. Why?

Then he knew. It was the woman's voice he'd thought he'd imagined. It was the voice that had told him, "Everything you need is inside of you."

"Samuel," the voice said again, this time out loud. The woman reached an arm toward him and beckoned.

Compelled, he left his father where he lay unconscious and moved forward. As he drew close, the shimmering figure clarified until he was able to make out facial features. Features very like his own.

"Dory?" It came out like a question, but it wasn't. This

was his mother. A lifetime of not knowing her fizzled as if she'd always been with him, as if she'd never left.

She smiled as he peered at her face: her nose, her chin. He reached to touch but found he could not. His fingers waved through mist.

"How is this you?" he asked. She appeared to be floating before the dark line, which he could now see was a chasm.

"It is the Wise One!" Flum cried and looked at Sam in wonderment. "The Wise One is your mother?"

Dory smiled at Flum and turned back to Sam. "We don't have much time, my son. You have questions."

"Yes, but—" A different panic overwhelmed him. "What do I ask first?"

She looked sad. "You want to know why I left?"

"Yes," he choked. "I mean, I want to know what all this is," he made a sweeping motion with his hand, "but let's start with that."

"To explain well would take more time than we have. The short answer is that I left to protect you. And magic."

Flum had told him their Wise One hid out on Osborne to protect someone. "Me?" he squeaked. "But magic isn't real!" The words sounded extra strange given the vision before him. "It's just science we don't know yet…isn't it?"

"Magic is real, my son."

He gulped. "Like what Flum and I did with moving doorframes and dirt?"

Her eyes flared. "So it is true. You are the one."

"What's true? What *one*? And what does protecting me have to do with protecting"—he gulped again—"magic?"

Her eyes lost focus and her lips moved soundlessly. Sam wondered if she was praying. After a moment she nodded and continued. "The women in our family line have protected old magic since the Northmen first settled Iceland. We, and women from three other branches in our family, are called the Sisters of Saemunder."

That name was familiar, thanks to Flum.

"Things have not gone well for us because of this. There was a time we were persecuted as witches, and so we hid. For your lovely father, and for you, I denied my heritage for many years until I could no longer. I followed my path."

"To Osborne," he said. "I still don't get why you had to leave."

"Patience." She looked beyond him as if there was someone just there. He turned and saw nothing but a shimmering mist that distorted the familiar edges of Omega Park.

"There once lived a dark sorcerer who sought to obtain a book of magic so powerful it might change the nature of the universe. In so doing he would turn magic in on itself, destroying it for all but one user. Him." She looked angry. "His spirit was imprisoned at the bottom of a lake. However, his return is foretold. As was your birth."

"I was—" He shook his head, willing his brain to catch up with his ears. "Foretold? As in a legend?"

"He will come for the grimoire he was denied, and then he will come for you."

"Grimoire? You mean like a magic book?"

"A powerful book of spells."

A bolt of alarm shot through him. "Why me? Why am I foretold?"

"You have the power to vanquish him forever."

He felt like his head was about to pop off. Every question led to more! "What power? The power Flum and I had is gone!"

She looked anguished. "I have not prepared you. I removed myself so that he could not track you through me. We hid you in a town no one knows about. Even Great-Aunt Halla, who dearly wished to know you, avoided using your name when she wrote." She smiled. "Yes, I knew she wrote. But there is magic in words, my son. She feared using your name would draw the evil one to you."

"You should have stayed," Sam choked. "We missed you, even though I don't even know you."

"I am so very sorry. At the time I felt it was the only way to keep you safe. This was my choice, and possibly a terrible mistake," she said gravely. "This breach through Odal Park is concerning."

"Odal? As in the ancient rune?" It was what Dennis said the park was called before it was changed to Omega.

Dory smiled. "Help will come, and you will learn all you need. Until then you must remain hidden. If he does not succeed in his quest before the winter solstice, his spirit will return to his watery grave. Until a next Son of the Solstice is born."

Son of the Solstice?

He felt frozen—like when he'd seen the image on the Icelandic database for the evil sorcerer. If only Flum could pull the plug on that memory just as he had the computer. In a weak voice he asked. "The dark sorcerer…is he in our family?"

She reached out a hand to him, and then lowered it as if remembering that she wasn't really there. "No, my son. Be calm. I have surrounded you with magical staves, but your greatest protection is within."

"We found the one under my skin. I thought it was

because of the lightning, but—" he shook his head in wonder. "I was born with it?" For a split second she looked confused. Did she not mean the image on his back? "You're telling me magic is real? Really real?"

"Yes, Sam. Really."

"And I'm some sort of superhero?"

"No, Sam. You are the foretold Son of the Solstice who is—"

"Yeah, yeah, destined to defeat some galactic bad dude. It's just that...*magic*?"

"Yes, Sam. Your whole life has been surrounded by it. You just didn't know it." She glanced toward where Dad had crumpled and now stirred. He moaned and rubbed his eyes.

"I will return and explain fully once I re-establish the shift."

"But it's broken. We couldn't find all the pieces."

She shook her head. "That wasn't it, Sam. That was a bypass I do not yet understand."

"Wait, what?"

She shimmered and turned to Flum. "Your Highness, it is time for you to come home."

"*Highness*?"

Flum shrugged then turned toward the chasm. "But I cannot float nor fly."

"You must help them, Samuel."

The wonder and terror formed a maelstrom that threatened to overwhelm him, but he understood. He must set aside his emotion along with his remaining questions about his destiny in order to help his friend. He'd promised.

"It's you and me, Flum. We moved the ground to make a tunnel. Together we can make a bridge." *Magic.* It hadn't been a shared electrical charge from the lightning. Magic was real. Really real.

He reached out his palm and waited for Flum to touch. He felt Flum's hand on his, but nothing else. No pulse.

It hadn't worked.

"It's too late," he choked. "Our magic is gone."

Flum shook their head. "You do not need me." They looked a little sad. "I did not help open the hole for your father. That was all you."

His mother spoke again. "Samuel, this is a time of great change for you. Believe, and be brave."

He felt something else then, this time from within. A vibration, like what he'd felt on his back after the imaginary ants were done. It began in his heart and shivered into other parts of his body. He closed his eyes to better feel. He put the palms of his hands together as if in prayer. The vibration moved from his heart to his spine and through his arms. When it reached his fingertips, he opened his eyes. He looked at the dark chasm, stepped forward and spread his palms wide and moved his hands as if rub out the empty space. As he rubbed the air, darkness was replaced by glowing light.

"You've done it!" he heard Flum whisper.

And so he had. Across the chasm there was now a bridge of gold.

"Time to go, young Royal," his mother said. The image of her began to lift and change.

"Wait!" Sam cried. "I need you to stay! Dad needs you too. We both miss you."

Once again, she looked beyond Sam to where Dad had fallen. Sam spun and saw his father sit up in the mist. He stared at Dory, eyes wide and mouth open.

"There is much to do," his mother said. Then, fully formed into the shape of a blue jellyfish, she rose high in the sky and was gone.

Flum had crossed the bridge and stood before the wall of light. They waved. "Goodbye my friend," they said.

A fat tear streaked down Sam's cheek.

Flum moved into the light and their shape got smaller and smaller until they were only a black dot. Then there were two black dots. One disappeared, and one grew. Soon it was a silhouette moving toward them.

"It's a person," Dad whispered. He was now standing beside him.

"It's not Flum," Sam said. The shape wasn't right. Nor the height.

The silhouette grew and grew, colours sliding and shifting in the dark, like rainbows on water, until it crossed the bridge and stood directly in front of them. The colours of the figure swirled, fast at first and then slower. To Sam it looked like something two-dimensional was birthed into three.

"Hi!" Thyla said.

Her face scrunched in confusion as she looked around the park. The rain had stopped, the cloud had split, and the sun shone once more. Sirens pierced the air and then cut, followed by a flurry of shouts as people rushed toward them.

"What's going on?" she asked.

CHAPTER NINETEEN

SPOOKY ACTION AT A DISTANCE

The next day was so normal that it felt weird.

Seconds after Dory and Flum returned to Osborne, Thyla had walked out of the mist as simply as if she'd been out for a stroll. The long cavern with the shimmery walls winked out and she'd asked, "Are you okay, Sam? I heard about the lightning."

Like when she'd disappeared, Sam was the only one who knew she'd been gone. Thyla had memories of the previous week as if she'd been in Gilla Farm the whole time. It was like her brain had filled in the gaps.

Sam accepted all of this calmly because he understood what had really happened. *Magic was real.*

Then corporals Joe and Sandy arrived and there was no more time to talk.

The mix-up with the RCMP officers was soon cleared up. Mr. Pockets was a witness to Dad's accidental punch, and the chaos at the detachment was also deemed an accident—which it most definitely was. Luckily, Corporal Joe's boss was able to sort through the confusion.

"But you know how it looked," Corporal Joe had said. The sergeant gave him a tired look.

Everyone decided that Sam's break-in at the Smiths had everything to do with his injury. He'd become confused and gone into the wrong house. He must have climbed in the window when his key didn't work, and after realizing his mistake had tried to jump back out.

"Yeah, that was it…hehe," he'd said, then added, "I'm really, really sorry."

No one brought up the stranger happenings at the RCMP detachment, specifically the whole walking through walls thing. Perhaps that memory had been wiped away as well. That or the lawyer and the dazed man in the interview room had made up other reasons for what they'd seen. Adults would always be good at that.

Dad believed everything, including the vision of Dory. That is, he believed it happened, and that there was a scientific explanation for everything. He was especially interested in what Flum told Sam about shifts and alternate worlds.

Sam couldn't wait to talk to Derek. *Hey, guess what, I have a superpower, and it's not invisibility!*

Except that after he'd made the bridge for *Their Royal Highness* Flum it had all fizzled out of him. There'd been no moving of matter, not even a vibration, no matter how hard he tried.

Dory had said she would return. Had she put on a set of magical brakes so that he didn't use his magic without knowing all its effects? He was dying to try again, which meant she was probably right to stop him.

Huh. That was a pretty grown-up thought, even if it wasn't all science and logic.

He frowned.

"Something wrong, Sam?" Dad asked.

"No. Maybe. It's just…is it okay that I believe in magic and you don't?"

"Are you asking if I disapprove?"

Sam nodded, but really he wondered if Dad would still like him if they thought different things.

Dad leaned back and considered. "One of the saddest and happiest days of my life was when I stopped believing in magic."

"I get why that's sad. Why happy?"

Dad grinned. "Because that was the day I found science."

Sam set a plate of stacked grilled peanut butter and cheese sandwiches on the table while Dad poured two glasses of milk. Sam breathed in the best smell in the world. He felt a pang as he remembered Flum's reaction to peanut butter and murmured, "Like Shnummy cake."

Sam reached for a sandwich and asked, "Have you figured out my tattoo?"

The rest of the feathery pattern on his back was fading, but the *Helm of Awe* remained. It looked like it had always been there—like a birthmark. That his mother had left that same stave on items in the house connected him to her in a way he did not yet understand.

"I know the area of science where it fits, but I need to research."

"It's magic," Sam said.

"Quantum physics," Dad insisted.

For Dad, science *was* magic.

Last night they'd sat up late drinking mugs of cocoa while Dad explained a part of quantum physics called "Spooky Action at a Distance." It had to do with things that were once physically connected but weren't anymore. He said that if you change something on one thing, the other thing will change too, even if it was on the other side of the world. Maybe in another world altogether. Was it possible that through this magical birthmark Dory stayed connected to Sam from Osborne, where she was a Sister of Saemunder protecting magic for the multiverse? Was that the reason he'd been able to do all those amazing things?

He looked at his hands. Never had two appendages looked more ordinary and powerless.

His mother was no longer "Dory" from a time long ago and far away. He'd seen her and had spoken to her. All the years Sam and his father had thought her missing, she'd been in Osborne, where she'd taught Osbornians about shifts and rune magic—like the translation pendant.

Those were the facts, but she'd left him with way more questions than answers.

"Dad, if Flum didn't get here through a shift, if it was a bypass like Dory said, does that mean there was never a shift between Earth and Osborne?"

"You want to know how Dory got to Osborne?"

"Well, yeah. It would have to be magic, wouldn't it?" He watched as Dad searched the corners of his brilliant brain for a scientific explanation. But there was something else bothering him. Something big. He now understood without a single doubt that he could tell his father anything, and yet he hesitated. Maybe because he knew Dad would not be able to logic it away. Of all the things Sam wanted to not be real, it was this. But it was too scary to keep it inside. He took a deep breath. Time for the final bug bomb of honesty. "Dad, Dory told me that the reason she left was to keep an evil sorcerer from finding me."

Dad paused with a sandwich raised halfway to his mouth. His eyebrows shot so high up Sam thought they might disappear into his hairline.

"She said that I'm a *Son of the Solstice*."

At that Dad nodded and chuckled. "Well, yes, you were born on the winter solstice. The rest is just…magical thinking—which is not the same as magic, which doesn't exist. Your mother always did believe in that kind of thing, but that's understandable because it's part of her heritage." Dad had begun to speak faster and faster, and his voice rose unnaturally high. "Did you know that there are still people in Iceland who believe in elves?"

"But Dad. If shifts, Flum, particle manipulation, and Dory travelling to alternate worlds are all possible, don't you think we should at least consider that this evil sorcerer might be too?"

Sam shivered, and Dad laid a comforting hand on his shoulder.

"If there is any science in this world that can explain this …story…your mother told you, I will find it. Until then, know that you are safe, and that I love you. I probably haven't said that enough, Samuel."

Sam grinned. "I love you too, Dad."

Sam was no longer invisible to his father. He understood that Dad loved *and* liked him. Sam loved and liked him right back. It didn't matter that Sam believed in magic and that his father did not. In his own special, if slightly uncoordinated way, Dad had stood up for Sam and stood *with* him in getting Flum back home. Together they were *Team Templeton*.

After lunch cleanup, Dad puttered in his garden while Sam went to his room to look up stuff on the internet. He wanted to know if the Icelandic database had any information about the old magic, and people like Dory: the magic keepers. He also wanted to research evil sorcerers, specifically the one who might come after him.

Correction. *Would* come after him. Of this Sam was certain. It really didn't matter if Dad figured out a scientific explanation.

He shivered and pulled on his favourite sweater—robin egg blue. It reminded him of Flum.

Something, a wisp of a memory tapped and then rubbed up against him like a stray cat seeking warmth and attention. He tried to shake it off—literally and figuratively. He could not. It had something to do with the database, something he'd seen during his previous search that hadn't fully registered. He pulled up his family tree and clicked on Dory's name.

As he scanned details, he thought about how the last time he'd done this Flum had been with him. He could almost smell the peanut butter.

Aha! There it was. Dory's birthplace was a farm called Gillastadir, in the region of Laxardal in Iceland.

*Gilla*stader. *Gilla* Farm. That was weird.

He put Gillastader through the online translation app. It meant Gilla Place. Dory was born on a Farm called Gilla Place. Or was it a *place* called Gilla *Farm*?

Super weird.

This was Spooky Action at a Distance times one hundred. Maybe even a million. It was also a mystery that must wait for another day. He'd had enough. It was time to be normal for a while, in his room surrounded by favourite and familiar things.

Sam remembered how Flum had explored his stuff with such interest and excitement. He was glad he'd given them his troll. It was something to remember him by. As he glanced his shelves, something hooked his eye. He looked closer but saw nothing out of place. He looked away, and out the corner of his eye again saw…something. It was more like a distortion, a "blink and you'll miss it" kind of thing. He tried again and had the same feeling.

Something was there, but not.

He stuck his hands in his pocket and whistled softly. He looked everywhere but at his target and took soft meandering steps around his room, as if sneaking up on a shy squirrel. There. Looking and not looking, as Flum had taught him, he sensed the distortion. At the last minute, he shot out his hand.

"Ow!"

He'd knocked something over. It was a book.

The cover was the colour of old parchment, like what he'd seen on the database page for the evil magician who was also his ancestor. Except instead of a hairy wolf-man, this picture looked to be an Icelandic rune-stave. It wasn't the Helm of Awe. He flipped open the cover and a bright light filled the room.

Everything began to spin.

The End

(for now)

AUTHOR NOTE

The runic symbols that appear on the title page are from the Elder Futhark. The title, *Peanut Butter and Chaos* translated into the Elder Futhark is ᛈᛖᚨᚾᚢᛏ ᛒᚢᛏᛏᛖᚱ ᚨᚾᛞ ᚲᚺᚨᛟᛊ. This translation was provided through the website valhyr.com.

In olden times before the development of our current written languages, there were runic systems. At the beginning of the Viking era, the Elder Futhark system was used. By the end, the more condensed Younger Futhark was common. "Futhark" is a word made from the first seven runes of this system, in much the same way we call our North American French- and English-language keyboards, "QWERTY."

THE ELDER FUTHARK RUNIC SYSTEM

Rune	*Phonetic Value*	*Name*
ᚠ	F	Fehu
ᚢ	U	Uruz
ᚦ	TH	Thurisaz
ᚨ	A	Ansuz
ᚱ	R	Raidho
ᚲ	K	Kenaz
ᚷ	G	Gebo
ᚹ	W	Wunjo
ᚺ	H	Hagalaz
ᚾ	N	Naudhiz
ᛁ	I	Isa
ᛃ	J	Jera

ᛇ	I/EI	Eihwaz
ᛈ	P	Perdhro
ᛉ	Z	Elhaz
ᛊ	S	Sowilo
ᛏ	T	Tiwaz
ᛒ	B	Berkano
ᛖ	E	Ehwaz
ᛗ	M	Manaz
ᛚ	L	Laguz
◇	NG	Ingwaz
ᛞ	D	Dagaz
ᛟ	O	Othala/Odal

TAKK

This novel is a departure from earlier works which may have been mythical and magical in moments, but not in genre. As always, it takes a village. I am blessed to have many supportive friends and family members who wrap me always in a warm embrace of wonder, kindness, and hope. Many helped with specific elements of this novel. I've applied their knowledge as best my oft-muddled brain could manage. All errors are my own.

My heartfelt gratitude to:

My family, Jim, Erin, Sara, Bob and Cathy, Heather, Merry, and Auntie Sharon, for never-ending encouragement. Extra thanks to Sara Daher for the title inspiration, and to Erin Daher and Jerritt Lipski for that hot summer day we hung out at my campsite and spitballed ideas. I would never have found the heart of this story without you.

Derek Mah for helping me understand how Sam might see a pixelated world.

Kevin (with mom, Judy) who stopped by one day on a school mission and said he would most definitely read a novel like this. Kevin, your enthusiasm put boosters in my rockets and encouraged me to finish this book.

Cam Patterson, fellow novelist, film collaborator and friend, for helping me see how a portion of Sam's journey might be adapted into a short film.

Cousin Kent Björnsson, for Icelandic language translation.

Sgt. Paul Manaigre, RCMP Media Relations Officer, for clarification on rank.

Friends and neighbours whose names I borrowed for characters (surprise!). A reminder that this is a work of fiction, and characters depicted are not real. Using your names gifts me a quiet smile as I remember you and your significance in my life.

Teresa and Joan, my high school "partners in crime" who with me all those years ago managed to register punk rock superstar John Lydon for a class and keep that bit of fun going until that fateful day with a voice came over Mr. Sigstad's classroom loudspeaker asking if this student had attended his class.

The Manitoba Arts Council and the Winnipeg Arts Council for financial support.

Agents Carolyn Swayze and Kris Rothstein, and the team at Great Plains Publications/Yellow Dog—Catharina, Mel, Sam and Keith—for believing in me, and *The Mythic Adventures of Samuel Templeton.*

The adventure continues.